Her emotions ran riot; his kiss was heavenly

Finally he pushed her away. "I think that's enough—for now. For a girl who didn't want to be made love to, you certainly did a quick turnabout."

She said tightly, defensively, "I expect you have no trouble in making anyone give in to you—sooner or later. You've got your own way with Liz and now you're trying me out."

"If I weren't a gentleman," he gritted, eyes blazing, "I'd hit you!"

"A bit too near the truth, am I?" Debra goaded. "Never put your hands on me again, Vane Oliver. You've had all you're ever likely to get from me!"

The fact that his kisses had thrilled her made her all the more angry. She had weakened, allowed herself to be swayed by this man. But there was no future in it. It had to stop—right now.

Divided Loyalties

by

MARGARET MAYO

Harlequin Books

TORONTO • LONDON • LOS ANGELES • AMSTERDAM
SYDNEY • HAMBURG • PARIS • STOCKHOLM • ATHENS • TOKYO

Original hardcover edition published in 1981
by Mills & Boon Limited

ISBN 0-373-02474-6

Harlequin edition published May 1982

Printed in U.S.A.

CHAPTER ONE

VANE OLIVER was every bit as intimidating as Debra had been warned. He sat on the other side of the desk, a giant of a man, wide-shouldered, thick dark hair, eyes that seemed to be permanently half closed making it difficult to read what was going through his mind.

She had the uneasy feeling that he was mentally undressing her and wondered whether she had done the right thing in coming for this interview. She hoped he was not fancying his chances with her.

It would be easy, she thought, too easy in fact to fall for a man of his fatal charm. He exuded a mysterious sexuality that was impossible to dismiss, and she felt herself wondering what it would be like to be kissed by him.

The next moment she pushed all such traitorous thoughts to the back of her mind. She was here after a job, not an affair.

'I'm very impressed with your qualifications, Miss Delaney. You appear to be exactly the person I'm looking for. Tell me, why are you giving up freelancing?'

Debra lifted her slim shoulders, her brown eyes candid. 'I wanted something more permanent, it's as simple as that.'

He nodded thoughtfully. 'You are familiar with my creations? You will be able to adapt your perhaps somewhat ultra-modern ideas to fit in with my image?'

She looked at him sharply, suspecting sarcasm, but his hooded eyes gave nothing away. 'Your dresses, Mr Oliver, are very individual, the embroidery detail superb. What woman would not recognise them?'

She had thought to flatter him, but his handsome face remained unmoved. 'These accessories, these belts and bags and gloves—I want them to be as individual as my clothes. You think you'll be able to conjure up some good ideas?'

'But of course, Mr Oliver. I wouldn't have applied for the job if I hadn't thought myself capable.'

Thick brows moved smoothly upwards, winging away into the thatch of hair that fell across his broad forehead. 'Confidence in oneself is a fine virtue, let's hope you live up to it.'

Debra went suddenly limp. 'You mean I've got the job?'

His full lips smiled for the first time since their meeting. 'Let's say I'll give you a trial. Three months on either side, how does that sound?'

'Oh, wonderful, Mr Oliver, simply wonderful!' Debra could not contain her pleasure. She needed a steady income now that she had Liz to look after, and securing this job at Vanoli was more than she had dared hope.

Her brown eyes shone and she stood up, slim and vibrant, full of energy. 'When do you want me to start?'

He was amused by her exuberance, making her realise that she was in danger of ruining the impression she had tried to give of a confident, self-assured young business woman.

'You can start on Monday,' he said. 'I shall

expect you here at nine prompt, I can't stand people who are late.'

'I'll be here,' she said. 'Thank you, Mr Oliver, I'm sure you won't be disappointed by your decision.'

As she prepared to leave he added, 'Oh, by the way, my secretary will give you a form to fill in. A pure formality, you understand, for the records.'

Debra could not wait to get home to tell Liz all about her new job. 'He's the most fantastic-looking man,' she said, 'but I wouldn't trust him an inch. Not that I expect much trouble in that direction. I suspect his sights are set much higher than the likes of me.'

Liz, seventeen and still at school, tried to be as enthusiastic over her friend's new job as Debra, but failed miserably. 'I'm pleased for you,' she said. 'I hope you make a go of it. Now, I'm going to my room to do some homework.'

Debra made no attempt to stop her. She knew that the homework was an excuse. Liz wanted to be alone; she had been like that ever since her parents died in a tragic road accident a month ago.

They had become friends in Hong Kong many years earlier, when both their fathers worked in one of the hospitals there. On returning to England Debra's father had immediately been offered a post in San Francisco. Debra had stubbornly refused to go, stating that she wanted to go on a course at the Royal College of Art.

Liz's parents had invited her to live with them, and for the last few years that was how it had been. Debra visited her own parents as frequently as holidays and finances permitted, but her permanent home was with the Freemans.

She had grown to regard them as family, and Liz as a younger sister, and she had been as heart-broken as her friend when Mr and Mrs Freeman died. She vowed there and then that she would look after Liz, try to repay in some small measure the love and affection her parents had given her.

This job meant that they could stay on in the house, they had no need to worry financially. Naturally Liz had inherited her father's estate, but his savings were in trust for her until she was twenty-one.

Debra was disappointed that Liz was not as excited as herself over the job, but knew that it was a question of time before the younger girl got over the tragedy that had so affected her life.

The next morning, which was Saturday, Debra was astonished to receive a phone call informing her that Mr Oliver wanted to see her again. No reason, nothing, except that he had requested her presence.

Debra felt faint annoyance. It could only mean that he had changed his mind, and if so why hadn't he told her yesterday instead of boosting up her hopes?

Recalling his preference for punctuality, she hurriedly dragged a comb through her short dark hair, dabbed powder on her cheeks and decided it would do.

The house of Vanoli was a bus ride away and she had to wait for a second bus when the first was filled with morning shoppers. Consequently by the time she reached his office she was breathless and flustered and not a little annoyed—nothing at all like the calm front she had shown yesterday.

She noticed that her form was on the desk before him and he looked at her with rather more interest.

What was wrong? He had said it was a pure formality. She knew that forms were usually filled in before a person was given a job, but it was his fault that she had not done so, why hold it against her now?

'Is something wrong, Mr Oliver?' she asked testily, when the silence between them had lengthened so as to be unbearable.

'This form,' he said, waving it in the air. 'You've amazed me, do you know that, Miss Delaney? You're a very talented young woman.'

'I am?' Debra's eyes widened. 'But you knew all about me before you took me on. Admittedly, I'm good at my work, I don't believe in hiding one's light under a bushel, but——'

He stopped her with a raised hand. 'I'm not referring to your qualifications. It's this that's taken me by surprise.' He stabbed a finger on the form and held it up for her to see.

Languages spoken, she read. Chinese.

'So?' she said impatiently. 'It's not a crime, is it? It so happens that I spent several years in Hong Kong when I was a child. Surely you're not going to hold that against me?'

'I see you have a temper too?' The grey eyes regarded her steadily and she felt suddenly uncomfortable, hoping that she had not jeopardised her job by her sudden display.

'I'm sorry,' she said quietly. 'I didn't intend to be impertinent, but I really can't see what it has to do with the job. I presume I still have it?' Her pretty round face was anxious, her eyes troubled.

He stood up suddenly, shocking her by his tremendous height. Six foot four, she imagined, wide-shouldered, slim-hipped, a perfect specimen of manhood.

'I have something better to offer you.'

His narrowed eyes watched her closely, trying to interpret her reaction, pausing expectantly.

She felt apprehensive, wished he would come to the point. Not knowing unnerved her, and this was not like Debra. Usually she was poised and confident; she had not got where she was today without a certain amount of business acumen too. But before this man she felt as uncertain as a schoolgirl. Her fingers twisted in her lap and she rose to face him.

'What is it you're trying to tell me?'

His smile was mysterious, twisting his full sensual lips, lurking in his dark eyes. She had the impression that he was enjoying this moment, liked the feeling that he was on top.

'I came for a job as designer of your accessory range. I'm not sure I want anything else.'

The full charm of those deep dark eyes was turned upon her. 'I'm sending you to Hong Kong.'

'You're what?' Her normally low-pitched voice rose by several octaves.

'I think you heard.'

'But what for?—I mean I can't, I mean—what do *you* mean?'

He touched her shoulders, pushed her down into the chair she had vacated. 'I've a branch out there and I've been looking for someone like you. You're just the person. You know the country, the language, the people. You're perfect. I——'

Debra pushed herself up angrily. 'It's impossible, Mr Oliver, I'm sorry. If I'd wanted a job in Hong Kong I'd have applied for one. Besides, I don't like my life being organised for me.'

Their eyes met in a battle of wills. Unflinchingly she stared back, and felt the full force of those silver grey eyes.

'Very well, Miss Delaney, will you work for me in Hong Kong?'

For another long minute she held his gaze. 'No!' she said at length, quite loudly and quite adamantly. 'It's out of the question.'

'Why?' he barked. 'According to this,' he picked up her application form, 'your parents are in San Francisco. What's holding you here? I'm prepared to offer a very generous salary and there'll be a flat thrown in.'

'Because,' she said, quietly now, 'I have commitments here. I can't leave England. Let's leave it at that, shall we?'

'What commitments?'

'Personal.' She did not see that it was any business of his.

He frowned angrily. 'Boy-friend?'

She shook her head.

'What, then, for pity's sake? I thought you'd jump at the opportunity. It's not every day a girl gets offered a job abroad, all expenses paid.'

It was tempting, she had to admit. She loved Hong Kong, found the different way of life exciting, and would enjoy going back. But how could she leave Liz? Had this happened before the accident she would not have hesitated, but Liz needed her now. There was no one else she could turn to, no aunts or uncles or cousins. Debra was all the 'family' she had.

'If you must know,' she said savagely, 'I'm looking after a young girl. I've known her many years. Her parents died recently and she has no one but me. I can't leave her to fend for herself.'

'How old is she?' The question was growled, as though it annoyed him to think that she was not a free agent.

'Seventeen,' supplied Debra.

'Old enough to look after herself,' he snapped to her astonishment. 'I thought you meant a child.'

'She is a child,' insisted Debra angrily. 'She's still at school. You're inhuman if you think she could look after herself.'

'I've known girls her age get married,' he said stubbornly.

'You don't know Liz,' retorted Debra. 'Her parents have sheltered her, she's immature for her age—she needs me.'

'And I need you,' he growled. 'Doesn't that mean anything?'

Debra decided he was making a fuss over nothing. 'I haven't known you all my life, Mr Oliver. I feel indebted towards Liz. Her parents took me in when mine went to America. Looking after Liz is the least I can do to repay their kindness.'

'And in a year or two's time she'll get herself married without giving you a second thought. Don't be too sentimental, Miss Delaney, it doesn't always pay off. I judged you to be a good business woman—was I mistaken?'

She shrugged. 'I have my loyalties. It's unfortunate that they happen to clash with your offer.'

'I'll increase your salary,' he said, and mentioned a figure which astonished her. She did not consider herself worth it. But it could make no difference. Liz was her first consideration.

'I'm sorry,' she said, 'no matter how much you offer I still shan't go. If it means I lose the other job as well, so be it.' She walked towards the door. 'It would appear we're both wasting time.'

He was there before her, tall and impregnable, vitally alive. His dark suit sat easily on wide shoulders, his strength of character hard to deny. How could anyone pit themselves against him?

Vane Oliver was tough and hard. Even Debra, who had never met him, knew exactly what sort of man he was.

And right now he wanted her to work for him in Hong Kong.

How was she going to make him give up? 'Excuse me,' she said, standing a few inches away from him. At five feet two she was compelled to tilt her head to look into the angular face. His cheeks were hollowed, as though he worked too hard and ate too little, she thought inconsequentially. 'I'd like to go. I think we've said all there is to say.'

Silver-grey eyes glinted from beneath lowered lids. 'You don't know me, Miss Delaney. I always get what I set my mind on.'

'So I believe,' tilting her chin defiantly. 'But perhaps you haven't heard about me. Once I make up my mind there's no changing that either.'

He smiled suddenly, surprisingly, but there was no humour on his face. Debra saw it as malicious and felt fingers of apprehension curl inside her stomach.

'We'll have to see who's the stronger of the two,' he said calmly. 'Dare I say, may the best man win?'

His calm assurance that he would end up winning changed Debra's fear to anger. 'You're so cocksure of yourself, Mr Oliver. I wonder how it will feel when you find yourself on the losing end for once.'

'I shan't lose,' he said calmly, moving away from the door and half filling two glasses from a decanter which stood on a table nearby. 'Here, see if this will help calm you down. You're like a prize turkeycock ready for battle.'

Normally Debra did not drink, but she was so enraged she took the glass and swallowed the contents. The neat whisky burned her throat. She choked and spluttered and, embarrassed, tried to turn it into a cough.

'Purely out of curiosity,' she said, 'what sort of a job is it that you're offering me? Not that I have any intention of changing my mind, you understand?'

'But of course,' he said politely, smiling to himself, confident now that the battle was half won. 'It will be very interesting work, involving meeting the many people who make up my garments. This branch covers the lower end of my range. Labour is cheap out there, my costs are greatly reduced, but I need someone who can speak the language. We've had a fair amount of trouble through them misinterpreting our instructions. This is where you would come in.'

It sounded good, interesting, and a sliver of doubt passed through Debra's mind. Could she leave Liz? The answer was immediate. No way could she let the younger girl look after herself.

He saw her hesitation. 'Naturally I wouldn't expect you to give up designing, after all that's what you've trained for, but I have no doubt that the two jobs could be combined. Does it appeal?'

She stared at him for a few long seconds, her

brown eyes wide. 'To be perfectly honest, Mr Oliver, it does. But like I said, I have this problem.'

'Problems can be overcome,' he said airily. 'Find someone else to look after the girl. There are plenty of people who'd be glad of such work. I'll pay the expenses, if it worries you.'

Debra's fine brows rose. 'You want me so badly?'

Sudden anger tightened his face. 'I don't like my plans thwarted,' he rasped. 'What's it going to take to make you change your mind?'

'Nothing,' she said tightly. 'Nothing at all, Mr Oliver. You're wasting your time.'

He leaned back against his desk, hands behind him. 'You're more stubborn than I realised. But what I don't think has occurred to you is that you're throwing away a chance in a lifetime, simply because of some stupid little notion that you owe this girl something.'

Was there to be no letting up? What was this man made of, iron? She sighed deeply and unhappily. 'Liz has enough troubles at the moment, and I'm certainly not going to contribute to them by jetting off to the other side of the world.'

His fingers strummed a quick tattoo on the edge of the desk, grey eyes flashed fire. 'Then take the damned girl with you if it means so much.'

A long silence followed, Debra not at all sure he meant what he said.

'Did you hear?' he questioned at length.

She nodded slowly. 'Why?'

'Because I've made up my mind that you're the right person for the job.'

'And you don't like to admit failure?'

'I haven't failed,' he said bluntly. 'The matter's

settled, the only difference is your friend will be going with you.'

Debra's chin shot up. 'I still haven't said yes.'

'But you will,' came the confident response. 'Has she a valid passport?'

The matter was being taken out of her hands and Debra did not like it. 'I believe so—but——'

'There are no buts,' he said firmly, taking her arm and ushering her towards the door. 'I'll be in touch. Be prepared to go almost immediately.'

Somehow she found herself outside his office wondering whether she had dreamt the whole thing. She felt as though she had been put through a washing machine, limp and wet, nothing like her normal self.

She was delighted to be going to Hong Kong again after all these years, especially as it meant she could still carry on with the work for which she had trained. It would have been a pity to waste all those years in college.

But it was Vane Oliver's attitude she was not keen on. He had decided that she was the person he wanted and that was that. It had been unthinkable that she might refuse. Contrarily now she wished she had been more firm. It would serve him right to have his plans thrown back into his face.

Debra did not immediately tell Liz the news. For one thing she was not sure how her friend would take it, and for another, she wanted to savour to herself for a while the idea of flying off to the other side of the world.

She felt quite exhilarated, annoyed as she was with the way Vane Oliver had handled the matter. A new job and a new country, it was more than she had ever hoped. Freelancing had been all right, but she had never been sure when she would get work. People were wary of someone fresh from college, not altogether convinced that she was capable of designing exactly what they wanted.

Mr Oliver, though, had seemed to think she was ideal. She suddenly felt ten feet tall, despite the fact that she had been bludgeoned into moving.

Unable to contain her feelings any longer, she called Liz from upstairs.

The girl came sulkily into the room. It was rare that she smiled these days, thought Debra, keeping her fingers mentally crossed that the news she was about to impart would cheer her up.

'How would you like to go to Hong Kong again?' she asked brightly.

For just a fraction Liz's eyes lightened, apparently recalling the years she had spent there as a child. But after a few seconds' silence she said flatly, 'No, I want to stay here.'

'But why?' insisted Debra. 'It will do you good to get away. There's too much here to remind you of——' she trailed away awkwardly.

'Of Mummy and Daddy,' cried Liz. 'That's why I must stay. I want to remember. I don't want to go away and forget them—it wouldn't be right.'

'You won't forget them,' said Debra gently. 'Not ever. But memories will be less painful out there. I think they would like you to go. You know how happy they were in Hong Kong.'

Liz wavered, and Debra pressed home her advantage.

'It's not going to cost us a penny. Mr Oliver is sending us. He wants me to work for him there, instead of here in London. He says you can come too.'

Liz looked up sharply. 'Why me? He doesn't know me, he has no reason to let me go too. What have you been telling him?' Her pretty baby face was flushed and she pushed an agitated hand through her long blonde hair.

Debra shrugged. 'I merely said I couldn't accept the job. He pressed for a reason and I told him about you. He's a kind man,' she lied. 'He immediately said we could go together. He's even finding us somewhere to live, rent-free. It's a chance in a lifetime, Liz. Do say yes.'

Liz said sharply, 'Do you fancy him? Is that the reason why you're so eager for me to go too, so that you won't lose the job. What would happen to me if you got married? Tell me that. I'm not stupid, you know. There has to be some good reason for you to be so insistent.'

Not for one minute had Debra thought Liz would feel like this. She had hoped she would be delighted, hesitant perhaps, but certainly not suspecting her of having fallen for Mr Oliver.

'Oh, Liz,' she said calmly, 'you do have some odd schoolgirl notions. No, I don't fancy Mr Oliver. I can't say I even like him. But this job's too good to miss, it's far better than working here in England.'

'Well, I'm not going!' Liz was shouting now, really agitated. 'I would feel I was letting Mummy and Daddy down. You can't run away from memories, Debra. You have to face them.'

She had some funny ideas, decided Debra, but for the time being she let the matter lie. Perhaps given time to think about it Liz would change her mind.

But the whole weekend passed and there was still

no sign of Liz relenting. She spent most of the time in her room, avoiding Debra, coming out only to eat her meals and then maintaining a stubborn silence no matter how much Debra tried to draw her into conversation.

It worried Debra, seeing Liz like this. Before her parents' death she had been a cheerful young thing, full of life, always clowning. It was only lately that she had seen the sensitive, emotional side of Liz's nature, and she wished there was something she could do to help.

But the younger girl seemed intent on shutting her out. It hurt, Debra had to admit, it hurt like hell. They had been so close, almost like sisters. She had never dreamt that she would get so uptight about this suggestion that they move to Hong Kong.

So far as Debra was concerned it was a fresh challenge, exciting, the sort of thing she would thrive on, and she had been convinced that Liz would feel the same.

On Monday morning Liz went to school without even bringing up the subject again, and Debra knew there was only one thing for it. She would have to go and see Mr Oliver, tell him that she could not go to Hong Kong after all.

With a bit of luck he might still let her have the job for which she had originally applied. She could see no reason why not.

At nine o'clock she was outside his office, confident, not too worried. But a few minutes later she wished she had never come.

'It's all arranged,' he said crossly. 'You can't back down now. I've booked your flight.' His silver eyes flashed, lips grim.

'You didn't know definitely that Liz would go,' she retorted, her brown eyes equally fiery. 'You might have waited until I'd given you confirmation.' He was so annoying, this man, always believing that people would do exactly as he wanted, without giving any thought at all to their own feelings. He was too bossy by far; perhaps it was as well that she was not going to Hong Kong.

'I didn't expect any trouble,' he said, leaning back in his chair, his whole attitude one of total aggression. 'I'm not accustomed to opposition to my plans.'

Debra almost said, 'I can see that,' but if she wanted this job in England she had to be careful. 'I'm sorry. I can't do much about it, though—Liz was adamant.'

He shook his head savagely. 'I thought she was in your care. Surely, if that's the case, she'll do as you say. Perhaps you weren't persuasive enough, Miss Delaney. I think you ought to try again.'

'It wouldn't do any good.' Debra stood up angrily. 'She's been through a traumatic experience, Mr Oliver. She's just lost all the family she's ever had. It's only natural she wants to remain here and preserve their memory.'

'It's morbid,' he returned tightly. 'It would do her a power of good to get away. Tell her she's going, make her go. My God, anyone would think you were frightened of the girl!'

'I care for her,' sighed Debra, 'that's the difference. I could no more force her to do anything against her will than I could——' She searched wildly for a comparison.

He finished for her, 'Have an affair with me?'

His suggestion shocked her, made her wonder

exactly what thoughts were going through his mind. Unless he was teasing? But there was no amusement on his face.

She said tightly, 'That's right, Mr Oliver. The two are both equally improbable.'

He pushed back his chair and came round the desk, standing a few inches away. 'You're twenty-two, Miss Delaney, ambitious, intelligent, a career woman in every sense of the word. Are you going to allow a seventeen-year-old girl to hold you down?'

His close proximity unnerved her. She stepped back a pace, trying to escape the indomitable strength, the rock-hard determination to get her to change Liz's mind.

'There's nothing I can do about it,' she said firmly. 'My first loyalty is to Liz. Surely there's some other person who can do this job?'

'I want you,' he said bluntly. 'I've made up my mind on that score,' and he turned on her the full power of his silver-grey eyes.

Debra felt herself turn to jelly. There had been more than a hint of double meaning behind his words. For as long as she could she held his gaze and then turning away said quietly, 'I suppose if I don't go to Hong Kong I don't get the other job either?'

'That's right,' he said tightly. 'Not that I shall be fortunate enough to find myself another designer who also speaks Chinese, but I feel there would be too much antagonism between us for a good working relationship.'

'In that case,' she lifted her slim shoulders, 'there's nothing more to be said. Goodbye, Mr Oliver,' and she held out her hand, trying bravely to hide her disappointment.

He ignored it. 'Goodbye is so final, Miss Delaney. I have a feeling that we shall meet again.'

It was quite conceivable, working in the same industry, she thought, but somehow she did not think that this was what he meant.

It was late evening when Debra returned home. Normally she tried to be in when Liz came from school, but somehow today she felt loath to face her friend.

Very faintly, and to her own alarm, she found herself blaming Liz. It was not Liz's fault, she knew. She could have gone to Hong Kong without her, but even so it caused a slight rift between them that had never been there before.

Consequently when she saw Liz's bright and cheerful face she was most surprised, and wondered what could have happened to bring about this dramatic change.

'I've had a visitor,' said Liz immediately. 'You'll never guess who.'

Debra frowned and shrugged. 'I've no idea, but I suppose you're going to tell me.'

Liz danced round the room, her blue eyes twinkling, looking more like her normal self than Debra had seen for a long time. Whoever it was they had certainly done her good.

Liz paused, made sure she had Debra's full attention. 'Mr Oliver,' she said importantly.

It took a full minute for Debra to comprehend exactly who she meant, then she said fearfully, 'Mr Vane Oliver? What did he want?' But she thought she knew even before her friend answered.

'He came to see me. No wonder you were so het up about getting that job! He's gorgeous, the dreamiest man I've ever seen. He made me feel so—so special.'

Debra knew only too well the effect he had, but Liz—she was too young, and at an impressionable age as well. She went quite cold at the thought of what this man had been doing.

'You still haven't said what he wanted.' Debra was becoming more anxious by the second.

Liz smiled mysteriously. 'He tried to persuade me to go to Hong Kong.'

It was what she might have suspected. It had been all too clear that he had not taken their parting as final. 'And what did you say?'

'I said yes,' said Liz pertly. 'If I'd known what he was like I would never have refused.'

Debra sincerely hoped that his methods of persuasion had been strictly above board. Liz had a starstruck look about her.

'In that case,' she said, 'I'm glad he came. I'd set my heart on that job, and I was terribly disappointed'

'So he said,' agreed the younger girl blithely.

'What else did he say?' asked Debra suspiciously, not at all sure she liked the knowledge that he had known what was going through her mind.

'Oh, this and that.' Liz seemed to take great delight in being secretive.

'He won't be going with us,' said Debra sharply, 'if that's what you're thinking. His place is here in London. Hong Kong is merely a branch. I suppose he goes out there occasionally, but, so far as I'm concerned, the less I see of him the better.'

Liz appeared about to say something and then changed her mind. 'That doesn't matter, does it?

He made me realise how pointless it was my remaining here. He said a change of environment
would do me a world of good.'

'That's what I said,' put in Debra sharply.

But Liz continued as though she had not heard.
'He said that Hong Kong has changed a lot since I
was there and that we'll be able to go places, meet
people. He made it sound exciting.'

I bet he did, thought Debra bitterly. Vane Oliver
would make anything sound exciting if it meant he
got his own way. But she hid her animosity saying
cheerfully, 'I'm glad, Liz. It's true, I'd set my heart
on the job. Thanks for saying you'll go.'

The next morning Vane Oliver telephoned her.
'Your tickets are ready,' he said bluntly. 'You'll be
travelling on Friday. Will that give you time to tie
up things this end?'

Too bad if it didn't, she thought acrimoniously.
'We'll manage,' she said coolly. 'But I don't know
what Liz's school is going to say about her shooting
off like this. She's studying for her exams. It will
ruin her education.'

His impatient sigh told her that he knew she
considered him thoughtless. 'I've already been in
touch with her headmaster, and he's given his okay.
As soon as she's settled I shall get her a private
tutor.'

'It would appear that money is no object to a
person like you,' she flung bitterly. 'I'm sure I can't
be worth all this trouble.'

'If you're not, I'm making a ghastly mistake,' he
said surprisingly. 'I'll be around to pick you both
up at ten on Friday morning, make sure you're
ready.'

The line went dead and Debra was left feeling that

she had fought a long battle and lost.

She told Liz the news when she came home, and was surprised to discover the girl already knew. Apparently Vane Oliver had told her headmaster the whole story and he had called Liz to his study, wishing her happiness in her new life, saying how fortunate she was to have a man like Vane Oliver take a personal interest in her education and welfare.

Some of Liz's initial euphoria had worn off, and sadness tinged her pleasure, but at least it had given her a new purpose in life, something to look forward to, and if she rather fancied the dynamic Vane Oliver—well, no harm would come from it. She would not see enough of him for him to have too great an impact.

CHAPTER TWO

I⊤ came as a considerable shock to Debra to discover that Vane Oliver intended accompanying them to Hong Kong.

He had called for them as arranged and driven to Gatwick airport, where she had fully expected him to take his leave.

But when he weighed in his own luggage along with their own she turned and said accusingly, 'Are you coming with us?'

'But of course,' came the prompt reply. 'I thought you knew.'

She glanced at Liz, who smiled selfconsciously. *She* knew, thought Debra. Why had she kept it to herself? Liz had said remarkably little about Vane Oliver since her first enthusiasm. This must have been why. She had been secretly hugging to herself the fact that she would see him again, afraid to say too much to Debra in case she decided not to go after all.

There was nothing she could do about it now, except keep an eye on her young friend, who was almost skipping with excitement.

It was difficult to hide feelings when one was young, thought Debra in faint envy. Liz had her whole future before her. Okay, it might have seemed like the end of the world when her parents died, but already she was beginning to emerge from her grief, soon they would be nothing more than a happy memory. There was so much to fill a young girl's life, grief and tragedy did not play too large a part.

So long as Vane Oliver did not figure too much in it, came the warning thought. Liz would need careful watching. She did not really think that the man himself would indulge in an affair with one so young, but Liz had a disarming manner. He could find himself involved without realising it.

He sat between the two of them on the plane, dividing his attention fairly, though there were times when Liz did all the talking. She was more excited than Debra could remember seeing her for a long time, and she was not altogether sure that their impending arrival in Hong Kong was the cause.

Vane Oliver was physically exciting and to someone as young as Liz he must seem the epitome of all that she ever desired in a man. Unless, of course, she saw him as a father figure, someone to replace her own dear father. But this was highly unlikely, judging by the stars in her eyes.

A sense of foreboding stole over Debra, and in an endeavour to attract some of his attention to herself she asked him to explain a little more about his branch in Hong Kong.

He seemed eager to comply. 'It's not a couture house in the strict sense of the word,' he said, 'because I have the work done in outside workrooms, unlike London where everything is done on the premises.

'Initially I thought this would be a good thing, but lately I've been having trouble. Quite often my instructions are misinterpreted. This is where you'll come in. I shall require you to visit the various factories, check that they're doing the work correctly, make sure everything is in order. With your knowledge of the language you should have no difficulties.'

It sounded interesting, but surely not so important that he could not have engaged someone else. 'Why couldn't you have employed a Cantonese?' she enquired. 'Many of them speak English, I'm sure they would have coped quite adequately.'

He shrugged. 'Maybe, but I'm not so sure. As a matter of fact, to be honest, I hadn't thought of asking anyone to do this work, I saw it as one of the hazards of the job. But when I saw your application form it occurred to me that you were just the person we needed—a very charming female troubleshooter, who will, I'm sure, have no difficulty at all in getting the workforce to eat out of your hand.'

Debra shot him a sidelong glance, aware that he was flattering her, but not sure that he was sincere. He could be shooting her a line for all she knew. He had managed to get her out to Hong Kong, now he must make certain she stayed.

Nevertheless his flattery was ego-boosting and she could not help feeling extraordinarily pleased.

They dozed off and on during the long journey, but as the plane approached Hong Kong Debra felt excitement course through her veins. It was inevitable that things had changed since she was last here, but from this height it all looked invitingly familiar.

The blue expanse of empty sea began to fill. There was Hong Kong Island, mainland Kowloon and the New Territories, the collection of smaller islands, and as they drew closer the scores of fishing junks and sampans—the immense floating towns which were as much a part of Hong Kong as the island itself.

The landing strip at Kai Tak Airport, on Kowloon side, jutted out into Victoria Harbour, built on reclaimed land, and as the plane made its dramatic sweep between the mountains and over the close-packed skyscrapers Debra closed her eyes. She always felt uneasy at this particular point, but once they touched down she could laugh at her fears.

She had been told, as a child, that the best way to arrive in Hong Kong was by ship at dusk when the early lights looked like jewels and the island itself seemed to be floating on a shimmering sea. Perhaps she might find time to take a boat trip this time and see this magical vision for herself.

Once off the plane and through Customs Vane Oliver ushered them into a taxi and soon they were speeding on their way.

Both Debra and Liz were entranced by the new tunnel that had been built beneath the harbour from Hung Hom in Kowloon to the northern shore of the island, and the journey which previously had to be made by ferry took no time at all.

Soon they were in the midst of skyscraper towers along the crowded waterfront. A smell of incense and oriental spices assailed their nostrils. They were back in the land they both loved.

Without giving them time to explore Vane Oliver headed straight for one of the towering office blocks near the harbour, where they were whisked skywards in a high-speed lift.

Vanoli occupied the whole of the top floor and they were met by a wizened Chinese with a white goatee beard.

'This is my business manager, Mr Fu,' said Vane
Oliver. 'Mr Fu, this is Miss Delaney, a new and
promising designer in the field of accessories, and
this is Miss Freeman, her young friend, who'll be
staying on the island with her.'

The elderly gentleman pronounced himself very
pleased to meet them. He spoke in slow, heavily
accented English, giving Debra an insight into the
difficulties Mr Oliver encountered.

Next they were introduced to Mai Mai. Mai Mai
was one of his chief designers, a very beautiful but
haughty Cantonese woman. She spoke little or no
English, but Debra had no difficulty in making
herself understood with her excellent command of
the language.

Mai Mai did not look too pleased at the thought
of another designer coming to work with them,
especially someone who appeared to be on very
close terms with Vane Oliver.

I wonder? thought Debra, qualifying herself with
the information that her talents lay in accessories
and not actual garments.

They were given tea and shown over the several
design rooms and showrooms, the airy, spacious
offices. To her surprise Debra found that she had
been allocated an office of her own.

'Does the job merit it?' she asked, wide-eyed.

'But of course,' replied Vane Oliver. 'You'll be a
very important person.' He looked down at her
warmly and Debra felt colour flood her cheeks. She
wished he hadn't the power to make her feel like a
jellyfish. It was those eyes that did it, half hooded,
mysterious, full of hidden meaning which you
could interpret whichever way you liked.

She caught Liz eyeing her speculatively and gave

herself a mental shake. It was bad enough Liz
fancying him without her doing the same!

'I think we'd like to go to our flat now, Mr
Oliver,' she said primly. 'Liz looks how I feel,
totally exhausted after that journey. A warm bath
and bed is all we want.'

A brief flicker, nothing more, crossed his face.
She could have imagined it. 'I'm sorry,' he said, 'I
should have realised, I ought to have let you
rest first. Mr Fu has my car waiting, I'll take
you.'

He drove in the direction of Victoria Peak—not
the highest hill in Hong Kong, but the most
famous, and where, Debra knew, the rich lived.

As they climbed, the skyscraper blocks fell away
beneath them. The China Sea looked almost purple
and the host of junks and sampans like toy models
on a lake.

They passed through dark patches of mountain
scrub, interspersed by white buildings, and very
soon turned into a narrow winding lane.

It must be some place he's taking us to, Debra
thought with growing suspicion, but it was not
until he stopped outside an impressive-looking villa
that her fears increased.

'We're to live here?' she queried doubtfully. 'Who
does it belong to?'

'It's mine,' admitted Vane Oliver calmly. 'The
apartment I originally had in mind was not big
enough for the two of you, and as this place can
adequately accommodate us all, I——'

Debra cut him short. 'I might have known! It's
my guess you had this planned all along!' She
returned to the car. 'We're not staying. Get back
in, Liz, this man's nothing but a scheming, low-

down, dirty rat!' She was so annoyed she could have
hit him.

But Liz had different ideas. 'You're a fool,
Debra. It looks marvellous. Where else would we
go? Rooms have always been short in Hong Kong.
We'd end up in some fleabitten shack. I vote we
stay.'

'You really have no choice,' added Mr Oliver,
watching her closely.

He was right, they hadn't, but it took a long
inner struggle with herself for Debra to admit it.
'We'll stay temporarily,' she said, 'until we can find
somewhere else. There is some other person living
in the house? We won't be entirely alone with
you?'

His lips quirked. 'Scared about your virtue? You
needn't be, you'll be perfectly safe. Lin Dai, my
housekeeper, will make an adequate chaperone.
Besides, no matter what you think, I'm not in the
habit of luring attractive young women into my
villa with the sole intention of seducing them.'

'The thought never crossed my mind,' flashed
Debra. But it had, and what was more annoying, he
knew it.

They passed through a walled courtyard with tubs
brimful of flamboyant flowers, peach trees, grotes-
que stone dragons. Liz gasped, admiring it all, but
Debra was too annoyed to give it anything more
than a cursory glance.

The house itself was single-storied with a curving
tiled roof and deep verandahs. It was in complete
contrast to the new villas and apartments, which
were like concrete boxes with square windows,
uninspiring, ordinary.

This villa had clearly been designed by someone

well versed in Chinese architecture. It was beautiful, and quite genuinely she envied him living here.

One could forget the hustle and bustle of the city, the overcrowded Chinese in their shanties and lean-tos. It was like an oasis in the desert.

Fleetingly she thought she would be a fool to give it up for a tiny apartment somewhere. But the idea of living with Vane Oliver, for however short a period, was abhorrent. Their stay must be temporary, even though she had practically fallen in love with the place.

Inside was as beautiful as out. Chinese furniture mingled happily with Western. Paintings by Chinese masters adorned the walls, precious Ming vases were displayed in glass-covered niches.

The girl who met them was dressed in the traditional *cheongsam*, the slim lines suiting her tiny body, the high side slits revealing neat shapely legs. Her dark hair was secured tightly at the back of her head, her slightly tilted eyes warm and smiling.

'This is Lin Dai,' said Vane. 'She'll make sure you're comfortable.'

Somehow he had given the impression that his housekeeper was an older woman, not this beautiful vision who could be no more than thirty. All Debra's misgivings returned and she glanced at her employer accusingly.

Forestalling her question, he said, 'I will get your cases. If there's anything you need you have only to ask.'

Debra clamped her lips. Liz danced on ahead, following the housekeeper along several corridors, clearly overjoyed at the thought of living in such a beautiful house.

Begrudgingly Debra followed. They were shown

to neighbouring rooms, each with a single bed covered in oyster-coloured satin, cool white walls and elaborately carved Chinese furniture.

'There's a shower room leading off,' the housekeeper informed them. Her English was a vast improvement on that of Mr Fu and unbidden came the thought that here was someone who could do the job she, Debra, was supposed to be doing.

But at least he had been truthful. He had admitted that the job of troubleshooter had been conjured up for her alone. She wondered why, why he had not been satisfied with her original application as a designer of his accessory range.

It did not make sense, but she knew there was no point in worrying about it—especially since it had meant her travelling out here. She loved the excitement, meeting new people, the fresh challenges. It was only Vane Oliver who caused her any unease.

The housekeeper continued, 'If you prefer a bath there is a bathroom along the corridor. Would you like something to eat before you sleep?'

Both Liz and Debra shook their heads. 'This is heavenly,' said Liz, stretching her arms gracefully above her head, unconsciously provocative.

Vane chose that moment to walk in with their cases, glanced across at Liz, eyes narrowed, then in a deliberately cheerful voice. 'Here you are, girls. Sleep as long as you like.'

He did not look in the least tired himself, which was annoying to say the least. Debra felt ready to drop and Liz had already sunk down on to her bed.

Both he and the housekeeper left and after ensuring Liz was all right Debra went into her own room. She took a quick shower and slid between the silken sheets, and in less than two minutes she was asleep.

To her amazement it was morning when she next woke. She felt better, completely refreshed—and ravenous. Popping her head round Liz's door, she observed that the younger girl still slept. She smiled fondly. It would do her good.

She washed and dressed in a short-sleeved cotton dress of lemon yellow which accentuated her dark hair and complexion.

From her window she could see down the slopes of the Peak, towering blocks that looked as though they had sprung up overnight, the intense blue of the China Sea.

Hong Kong had changed, she had realised that yesterday. There were parts she did not recognise, where old buildings had made way for new. It still teemed with life, however, was vitally alive, over-crowded, happy, feverish. Debra loved it.

More happy than she had felt before going to bed, she made her way along the corridors until she found the breakfast room.

Vane Oliver sat at the table, an open newspaper before him and the remains of his meal to one side. He was freshly shaven and wore a white silk shirt open at the neck, revealing the brown column of his throat.

He smiled warmly. 'You look better. How about Liz, or is she still sleeping?'

Debra nodded. 'I thought I'd leave her.'

He poured her coffee from an elegant silver pot, his smouldering eyes watching her closely. It felt far too intimate, she decided, sitting with her em-ployer like this. It was not at all what she had expected, but it was quite clear from his attitude that he was quite happy with the situation.

'One free day before you begin your job,' he said. 'What would you like to do? Renew acquaintance with Hong Kong? I can drive you and Liz around the island, if that's what you'd like. Or you can spend a lazy day here in the grounds. It's very pleasant.'

She took a long sip of her coffee before answering. 'I think I'd like to go and look for somewhere else to live,' she said firmly. 'Liz and I can't put on you for too long.'

His eyes hardened fractionally. 'That's nonsense. You're both welcome here for as long as you like, and you know it. Why don't you give up your idea of moving?'

'Because it's not right,' she snapped. 'I'm old enough to look after myself, but Liz is easily in-fluenced. You've already made quite an impression on her, in case you weren't aware of it. I don't feel that we should live in such close proximity. It can do nothing but harm.'

'I think we should let Liz speak for herself,' he said. 'She's not quite the ingénue you make out, I feel sure.'

Debra shot him a wide startled glance. 'What makes you say that? What were you up to that day you came to our house?' Her heart raced and every fear she had ever felt regarding this man came rushing to the surface.

'I'm not sure I like the way your mind works,' he said with swift aggression. 'Do credit me with more sense than to involve myself with someone half my age. What I'm trying to say is that girls of seventeen in this day and age are not the precious little virgins they were twenty years ago. They get around a bit, they see life. Half of them are more experienced, I would say at a guess, than you.'

Debra ignored the innuendo to herself. 'Not Liz,' she asserted stoutly. 'Don't forget I've lived with her most of her life. I know exactly what makes her tick.'

He smiled at her outrage. 'What interests me,' he said slowly, 'is what makes *you* tick. You're a funny mixture, half woman, half child. One minute all businesslike and self-assured, the next temper out of control and saying things that I honestly don't believe you mean.'

'Like what?' she demanded savagely.

'Like the fact that you think I'm a bad influence on Liz. Let me tell you here and now, Debra Delaney, that I have no designs on your friend. If she romances a little, sees me as some sort of glamorous figure—well, it can't be bad, can it? Especially if it will help her get over her parents' death.'

'And what happens when she realises her feelings are all one-sided? How do you think she'll feel then? No, Mr Oliver, I reckon the quicker we're out of here the better.'

'And I think you're exaggerating a situation that doesn't exist,' he retorted, quite angry now, his eyes more silver, his jaw firm. 'Liz is ripe for romance, I'll grant you that, anything to draw her out of her misery, but as for her and me, it's ridiculous, and you have nothing more to go on than your own unfounded suspicions. You also have my word that I won't lay one finger on her.'

Debra supposed she had to be satisfied with that, but it did not alter the fact that the sooner she was away from here the better. She would take every opportunity to look around for a place of their own.

They finished their meal in silence, Debra fuming inwardly over what she considered Vane's offhand manner. He seemed to think that she was making a fuss about nothing. He had no idea how she worried about Liz.

Vane left the room before her. 'Give me a shout if you want to go anywhere,' he said. 'I'll be around.'

She did not even bother to answer. If she had her way she would go nowhere with him. He had tricked them into coming here to his villa and she was sure he had no intention of letting them go.

Quite what motive lay behind his planning she did not know, but it was not a situation which appealed to her. No man invited two girls to stay with him for no reason at all. He would need careful watching, especially where Liz was concerned.

Liz came in as she was about to leave, still wearing her nightdress over which she had slipped her dressing-gown. But it was unfastened, and Debra frowned.

'We're not at home now, Liz,' she said sharply. 'Please remember that there's a man in the house. Go and get dressed at once.'

Liz yawned and stretched and looked at Debra rebelliously. 'Don't boss me about, Deb. I'm hungry, I want my breakfast first.'

Looking at her friend, Debra thought it was a good thing Vane had disappeared. With her blonde hair attractively tousled and a healthy pink flush to her cheeks, plus the fact that her semi-transparent nightdress revealed a firm young body, he would undoubtedly have had thoughts that would bode no good for Liz.

'And I say get dressed first. For heaven's sake, Liz, you don't want Mr Oliver making a grab at you! Because that's what will happen, I'm sure. He's a virile man, but far too old, and don't you forget it.'

Dimples appeared in Liz's cheeks. 'I've already seen him. He gave me a good morning kiss, as a matter of fact.'

Debra's lips tightened. So much for his promise! 'You had no right letting him,' she said fiercely. 'Sit down. Just this once you can eat breakfast like that, but in future I insist you get dressed. Do you hear?'

Liz nodded and sat down sulkily. 'You spoil all my fun.'

'Fun!' exploded Debra. 'Playing around with the likes of Vane Oliver isn't fun—it's positively dangerous! You really irritate me, Liz. Only a few days ago you were still grieving, now here you are practically shoving yourself at my boss. I'm surprised at you, I really am. If your parents could see you now they'd give you the good hiding you deserve.'

Biting angrily into a piece of toast, Liz said, 'I still miss Mummy and Daddy like hell, but you keep telling me life has to go on, so I'm doing my best to snap out of it.'

'The transition period's so swift, though, Liz, I can't believe it. If you're putting on a face you're making a good job of it, but I don't think you are, you're not a good enough actress.

'You think you've fallen for Vane Oliver, I'm sure. It's something that happens to all girls your age—they fall in love with the unattainable, usually a pop star. But for God's sake don't throw yourself at him. That's no way to solve your problems, you're only inviting more heartache.'

Liz's eloquent blue eyes looked across at her friend. 'Vane and I had a long talk that day he came to the house. His own parents died when he was about my age, so he understands exactly how I feel. The only cure, he said, was to throw myself wholeheartedly into doing something. His ambition was to be a dress designer and he went all out to pass his exams and become a success.'

Debra eyed her steadily. 'And what did he advise you to do?'

'Firstly to get away,' replied Liz, 'and then to work as hard as I can at my school work. I told him I want to be a doctor, like Daddy, and he said he'll help me all he can.'

Hence the hero-worship, thought Debra sadly, wondering why he had been so kind to a girl he had just met. She wished she could believe it was an innocent relationship. A true friend like Vane would do Liz good, make up in some way for the loss of her father. But if he was playing about, if his intentions were less than honourable.... Debra clenched her fists and counted to ten.

'Finish your breakfast, Liz,' she said bitterly. 'I'll see you later.'

'Can we go out?' asked Liz eagerly. 'Vane said something about a tour of the island.'

Debra nodded. 'If you like.' But she could whip up no enthusiasm. She was annoyed with Vane for breaking his word and kissing Liz. She was annoyed with Liz for flaunting herself. She was annoyed with the world in general. What had promised to be an exhilarating change was turning into a nightmare.

While waiting for Liz she sauntered out into the

gardens. They were filled with beautiful flowers, hibiscus, coxcombs, pinky white bauhinias. Carp lay in the still silvery waters of a pool, swallows skimmed overhead. It was exotic and peaceful, but Debra's distress was not easily assuaged, and when she saw Vane sitting in the shade of a peach tree her steps quickened.

He looked up as she approached, smiling encouragingly, and her resolution faltered beneath the warmth of his gaze. She wished he were not so handsome, so capable of making a woman feel that she meant something special to him.

One look from those silver eyes and she went weak at the knees and it took all her willpower to maintain her anger. She flashed him a belligerent look. 'What do you mean by kissing Liz?' she demanded. 'You promised not to touch her.'

His thick brows slid up smoothly. 'Is that what she told you?'

'Are you calling her a liar?'

'Not in the least, but perhaps she's adept at twisting the truth.'

Debra frowned. 'I'm sure I don't know what you mean.'

He studied her for a few seconds. 'Your little friend kissed me. She came flying out of her room and almost knocked me over. Naturally I held out my arms to steady her, and the next moment her lips were on mine.'

'I don't believe you,' snapped Debra.

He shrugged. 'Believe what you like, it's the truth. Admittedly I got a certain amount of satisfaction from the feel of her body in my arms. What man wouldn't? She's—very attractive, your little friend. One day she's going to be a beautiful woman.'

She glared angrily. 'And you did nothing to stop her kissing you, after all I'd said about her having a crush on you?' The man was a beast, not to be trusted, not one inch.

'If you're trying to say did I encourage her,' he frowned grimly, 'no, I did not, but I couldn't hurt her feelings by rejecting her.'

'It would be better in the long run,' said Debra.

'She needs kindness at the moment,' he replied gently. 'She's still pretty much upset. All this pretence at gaiety is a front, she's trying to bluff out her sorrow. I think she's very brave.'

Recalling that he too had suffered a similar bereavement, Debra reluctantly conceded that he might be right. Perhaps he, strangely enough, understood Liz better than she did herself. But she was not prepared to admit this.

'I still don't like the way she's behaving towards you. I'd appreciate it if you didn't encourage her.'

Vane sighed impatiently. 'I'm not,' he said. 'I'm merely being friendly. Sometimes it's easier to confide in a stranger than it is to someone who's been close to you all your life.'

'I wish I felt as confident,' she replied, more calmly now. 'I'm worried about Liz, and——'

'Unnecessarily so,' he interjected, standing up and placing his hands on her shoulders. 'Dear Debra, relax, stop being over-protective. Take each day as it comes—and talking of today, have you decided what you want to do?'

His close proximity caused her breath to catch in her throat and Debra gave an angry shake of her head. She had never before met anyone quite like Vane Oliver. How a man she distrusted could have such an electrifying effect on her senses she did not know. It was disturbing to say the least.

'Liz wants to go sightseeing,' she said tightly.

'And you, what do you want to do?'

He made it sound as though it was important to him, and she tilted her head so that she could see his face clearly, then wished she hadn't as the intensity of his eyes seared through her, quickening her pulses and making her skin tingle warmly.

'I'll fall in with the majority,' she said, forcing lightness, wishing he would let her go. She could move, of course, quite easily, but that would give him the satisfaction of knowing that he disturbed her, and in no way was she going to reveal that.

He smiled slowly. 'You sound reluctant. A pity, I want you to enjoy the day. A happy beginning to our new association.'

Before she had time to realise what was happening he had kissed her, a brief hard kiss that shocked her so that she had no time to feel anything before he suddenly let her go.

'What did you do that for?' she asked, wide-eyed, a little bemused.

'Why does a man usually kiss a woman?' he countered. 'You've a very kissable mouth, Debra Delaney, in case you didn't know it.'

He seemed to have difficulty in tearing away his eyes, and Debra felt herself grow warm. She was under no delusion that he talked to all women in this way, and it was with relief that she saw Liz approaching across the lawn.

'What are you doing out here?' called the younger girl. 'I thought you'd gone without me.'

Vane looked at her and smiled. 'Admiring the view. Are you ready?'

Debra could have kicked him and scowled as she followed them back towards the villa.

His car was waiting outside the courtyard gates, and Liz climbed into the front without being asked. 'You don't mind, do you, Deb? You know how sitting in the back makes me sick.'

It was true, but by no means as bad as Liz made out. It was an excuse to sit by Vane, that was all, and if Liz thought Debra was not aware of it, then she wanted her head examining.

As they made their way down the Peak Liz kept up a constant stream of chatter. In a way Debra was thankful that all she had to do was sit back and watch the city loom nearer. She studiously avoided looking at Vane's reflection in the interior mirror, knowing full well that at times he purposely watched her.

The longer she knew him the more disconcerting she found him, and it irritated her that her new employer should have this ability to make her feel awkward.

Once they reached the crowded streets of Victoria Liz said impulsively, 'Oh, Vane, let's go shopping instead. I'd forgotten how exciting it all is. I was only a child the last time I was here, but I can still remember the smell of incense and the washing hanging over balconies, and the festivals and the neon lights.'

'You still are a child,' he teased.

Debra saw Liz's back stiffen. 'No, I'm not, I'm seventeen. In another six months I'll be old enough to vote.'

'So old,' he mocked, but the bantering light in his eyes soon had her smiling again. 'We can go shopping if you like,' he said easily. 'How about you, Debra, does it appeal?'

'I don't mind what we do,' she said politely, in-differently.

His eyes narrowed, but he parked the car and soon they were a part of the bustling city. They rubbed shoulder to shoulder with Chinese in black trousers and short jackets, dodged baskets of dried fish swinging from a pole, sniffed the new and ex-hilarating smells which were like a drug.

Before long Debra forgot her antagonism and became as intoxicated as Liz with the thrill of it all. She glanced curiously at an elderly Chinese man carrying a gilded cage with two tiny white birds whistling loudly, exclaimed over hundred-year-old eggs in the street market, and pointed out ducks that had been pressed as flat as pancakes.

'Anyone would think you girls had never been here before,' exclaimed Vane, smiling indulgently at their animated faces.

'It's been so long,' said Debra. 'Besides, you see things with different eyes when you're grown up. Oh, look at those poor crabs!'

A stall was piled high with crabs bound and gagged ready for the pot. Next to them were fish dried out like parchment.

They ate lunch at one of Hong Kong's countless restaurants and then continued their shopping expedition.

So far they had bought nothing, merely allowed themselves to be caught up in the magical spectacle of it all, sampling dried sea-horse from one of the many herbalists' shops, allowing Vane to introduce them to Chinese wine to which had been added snake venom. It was not until they had swallowed the contents of their glasses that he informed them that it was supposed to be an aphrodisiac.

Debra stared at him in horror, not really believing. Liz laughed happily. 'What a lucky man you're
going to be tonight!'

'That's what I had in mind,' he said solemnly,
and Debra could not be sure whether he was joking
or really meant it.

They got lost in the labyrinth of side streets,
enthused over exquisite Oriental jewellery, leather
goods and lamps. The variety of merchandise on
sale was infinite, and when Vane insisted on buying
them each a present Debra settled for a beautifully
carved ivory box, and was annoyed when Liz let
him give her a pair of gold filigree earrings set with
tiny pearls and jade.

'They're not real,' she said, when they got back
to the villa and Debra tackled her about it.

'That's beside the point,' argued Debra. 'No girl
accepts jewellery from a man unless he's someone
special.'

Liz's blue eyes flashed. 'Vane is special. He's
good to us, you can't deny that. He's the nicest,
kindest person I've ever met.'

And no amount of arguing is going to make you
change your mind, thought Debra, sighing inwardly
and leaving the other girl to take a shower and rest
before their evening meal.

Debra had not wanted to make a fuss in the
shop over the jewellery, but she intended speaking
to Vane about it all the same. He was giving Liz the
wrong impression, whether intentionally or not.

He had said dinner would be ready about seven.
At six-thirty she set out in search of him.

She found him on the verandah, eyes closed,
though she felt sure he was not asleep. He had

changed into a cream silk evening shirt and a pair
of dark slacks, and was half sitting, half lying on a
cane lounger cushioned with brilliant yellow pillows.

Deliberately making herself heard, Debra stood
over him. 'Mr Oliver, I want a word with you.'

No indication that he had heard.

'I know you're not asleep, so please don't pretend
you are!'

At the angry tone of her voice his lids flickered.
'Fire away, I'm listening.'

'Then look at me!' snapped Debra, wondering if
he was deliberately making things difficult for her.

'I am looking,' he said, and she realised that he
was watching her through the thick fringe of his
lashes.

There was a chair beside him and she sat down,
feeling that she could talk more easily if they were
on the same level. 'Why did you buy Liz those
earrings?' she demanded.

'Because she wanted them, isn't that a good
enough reason?'

She shook her head savagely. 'I don't agree.
Jewellery is personal, usually only given to
someone who's close to you.'

A slow smile widened his lips, annoying her even
more. 'What a sweet old-fashioned thing you are!
But it was a trinket, nothing more, something
pretty that Liz fancied. Surely you're not reading
anything more into the gift?'

'Knowing you, yes,' she snapped.

Very gradually Vane hauled himself up so that
he sat facing her. She was aware of muscles rippling
beneath the smooth silk of the shirt, and became
fascinated by the hidden power.

It was funny, she thought, she had always imagined dress designers to be dapper, effeminate men, nothing like this towering giant who could flatten her with one blow if he so chose.

'What do you expect me to do?' he snapped, features suddenly harsh. 'Ignore the child? Pretend she doesn't exist?'

'Now you're being stupid,' she cried. 'You know very well that's not what I mean, but you could try treating her as though she were a child and not some sex object for whom you've developed a fancy.'

'I don't think she'd thank me for that.' He pushed himself up and stood over her. 'Liz doesn't see herself as a child any longer, and neither do I. Maybe she was before her parents' death, maybe she's grown up quickly, I don't know, but I do know that she would hate it if I patronised her.'

'Mr Oliver,' Debra suddenly made up her mind, 'I don't think this Hong Kong thing's going to work out. I think we should go back to England now, before I begin the job, before I feel guilty at letting you down.'

'And what do you think Liz would say to that?' Eyes as hard as ice pierced her own.

'I don't suppose she'd like it,' admitted Debra.

'I know damn well she wouldn't,' he came back fiercely. 'Think about it for a minute, Debra. This trip out here is the best thing that's happened to her since the loss of her parents. By taking her back now you would be doing the harm. She'd withdraw into her shell, she'd resent you as well. Life wouldn't be worth living for either of you.'

He was right, damn him, but Debra was reluctant to admit it. 'Suppose we stay, then,' her chin lifted determinedly, 'what do you propose doing about your behaviour?'

'Precisely nothing, my dear Debra,' he said coolly. 'It's you who's worrying, not me, and I'm perfectly sure Liz isn't either. If I were you I'd push all this nonsense about me trying to seduce Liz out of your head. In the long run you'll see that you've been bothering about nothing.'

With those words he left her and walked back into the house, and there was nothing she could do except follow, admit defeat, and wait and see what happened next.

CHAPTER THREE

THE next morning Vane drove Debra down to the offices of Vanoli, leaving Liz still asleep. Cars and trams were nose to tail along the entire route, and it took them so long that Debra thought they would have been better off walking.

She did not speak, their affray of the day before still uppermost in her mind. Inside the building they each went their different ways.

She had scarcely seated herself when the phone rang. It was Vane. 'I'd like to see you in my office,' he said.

Why the hell couldn't he have mentioned it before, whatever it was? she pondered angrily. It was ridiculous him sending for her like this when they had only just parted.

But her frown faded when she saw the troubled look on his face. 'What's wrong?' she asked.

'I've just had a phone call from London,' he said. 'They've received a consignment of dresses from Yam Ling Kee with the wrong embroidery on. Why the hell no one checked them, I'll never know. But I want you to get over there right away, tell them what's happened, and insist that I have a new lot ready by this time next week. If not they lose my business.'

'A week's not long,' said Debra, 'don't you think you're pushing it a bit?'

'You're paid to do as I say,' he snapped furiously. 'My reputation is at stake here. Go now, take a taxi,

50

or get someone to drive you. I think it might be best if you had a car of your own. Send Mr Fu in, I'll ask him to see to it.'

This was the business side of Vane Oliver, demanding and expecting obedience to his wishes. Debra had no thought of defying him.

The company were all apologies for their mistake. It transpired they had used appliqué work instead of embroidery for the intricate details which were Vanoli's trademark. In actual fact Debra felt sorry for them. There was so much work involved. Surely it would not have mattered on this one occasion?

But clearly Mr Oliver was a revered person and in no way did they wish to lose his custom. 'We will do it,' Mr Ho, the young Chinese manager, assured her. 'No problem at all. Perhaps he will let us have the others back. We may be able to sell them elsewhere.'

'Not with Vanoli's label in,' said Debra sharply. 'He'd never forgive you.'

'I understand,' replied Mr Ho. 'We will cut them out, naturally.'

'Make sure you do,' she said sternly, 'if you value Mr Oliver's business, because if that lot get on to the market with Vanoli's label in there'll be hell to pay, and I'm not joking.'

'Do not worry, Miss Delaney,' he said earnestly. 'We will start work on the corrected garments straight away. Mr Oliver will not be disappointed.'

Rather pleased with herself for managing to sort out this, her first problem, Debra hurried back, only to discover that Mr Oliver had gone out, leaving a message to say that he would not be back that day.

Left with nothing else to do so far as her new job

of troubleshooter was concerned, Debra made her way to the showrooms, intending to study Vane's designs so that she would have a good idea of the sort of accessories he would need to go with them.

She had not been there long before Mai Mai came in from the design room next door, quite clearly with one purpose in mind – to find out exactly what Debra meant to Vane Oliver.

'I was surprised,' she said without preamble, 'to discover that Mr Oliver had employed a new designer. Have you known him long?'

Debra studied the other woman for a few seconds. She was very beautiful, with that tiny trim figure of all Chinese women. Her black hair was brushed back from her face, fastened with a cluster of pearls which matched the ones round her neck. Her expressive fingers were red-tipped, echoing the colour of the dress that she wore.

'I hardly know him at all,' admitted Debra, and thought she saw a flicker of satisfaction cross Mai Mai's face.

'Why has he brought you here?' continued the other woman. 'I did not know he had any plans to employ a new designer.'

Debra smiled. 'Actually I applied for a job in London. It was his idea, not mine, to bring me out here. I believe he sometimes has trouble with some of the factories, and as I speak Cantonese fluently he thought it would be a good idea if I made this my base, helping him out in that direction as well.'

'Quite an important job.' The words were said jealously, dark eyes flashing fire.

'I wouldn't say that,' shrugged Debra. 'But it certainly sounded exciting when he explained it to me. Have you ever been to England?'

Mai Mai smiled mysteriously. 'Not yet.'

But you're working on it, thought Debra. The designer was not all that clever in hiding her feelings. 'It's not so busy as here,' she said. 'I love it here, I'm glad to be back.'

Surprised, Mai Mai said, 'You have been here before?'

'Oh, yes,' replied Debra. 'I lived here as a child. My father was a doctor at the Queen Mary Hospital. That's how I learned to speak your language.'

'I thought that Mr Oliver seemed particularly friendly towards you.' Mai Mai continued her third degree into their relationship.

'I wouldn't say that,' shrugged Debra. 'He treats me much the same as he would any other new employee. Of course, I suppose it makes a difference living with him, but I wouldn't say we were close friends.'

If she had dropped a bomb Debra could not have caused more shock. Mai Mai's eyes widened and then narrowed angrily. 'You live with him? He did not tell me.'

'Why should he?' asked Debra, and then realised it was not the sort of question she ought to have posed. If Mai Mai were his girl-friend it could cause all sorts of unpleasantness.

'There is no reason why he should,' said Mai Mai, carefully controlling her anger, 'except that he does normally discuss things with me.'

Debra tried to placate her. 'It was all arranged very quickly. I don't suppose he had time. Besides, it's only temporary until we find somewhere else.'

'This girl, this other girl you had with you yesterday, who is she?' demanded the Cantonese woman imperiously.

Debra did not see that it was any business of hers, but rather than cause any further unpleasantness she answered coolly, 'She is my friend.'

'Why is she here?' snapped Mai Mai. 'Is she going to work for Vane too?'

'No,' said Debra, and saw no reason to elucidate further. Let Mai Mai think what she liked. Suddenly she did not like the other woman.

'I suppose,' said Mai Mai, abruptly changing the subject, 'that you and I will be working fairly closely together. Do you want to see some of the designs I am working on at the moment?'

There was no smile on her face and Debra guessed it was the nearest she would get to being civil. She nodded. '*Mm koi.* Mr Oliver left without giving me instructions. Perhaps I could work out a few ideas and surprise him.'

Judging by the expression on Mai Mai's face she did not think that a good suggestion, but then Debra hadn't supposed she would. Mai Mai would see it only as a way of gaining further favour with the man she was clearly half in love with herself.

Debra was entranced with the new designs. Vane had departed from his usual exotic embroideries, using instead thousands of tiny pleats—pleated skirts, sleeves, waistbands and cuffs, pleated collars, all using beautiful materials, silks and taffetas, chiffon and georgette, fine cottons.

Her mind worked overtime picturing the various accessories that could be worn with such entrancing, delicate garments. Strappy sandals in colours to match, belts so light and exquisite that they would look like part of the dress, doing nothing to detract from their ethereal beauty.

She thanked Mai Mai for letting her see the

sketches and hurried back to her office, pinning a
sheet of paper to the drawing board that had been
provided for her use, quickly sketching a few ideas
before she lost her initial impressions.

It came as a surprise when Fu Ju Wen entered to
say it was five o'clock and everyone was going home.

'I had no idea,' she said. 'I was so busy, time's
simply fled.'

'Would you like a lift?' he enquired in his courtly
manner.

She smiled and shook her head. 'I'll walk, it's
quicker. There's so much traffic it's unbelievable.
The poor rickshaws don't stand a chance these
days!'

He looked sad for a moment. 'Soon there will be
none. They're issuing no more licences. It is a pity,
a great pity.'

'An unfortunate part of progress,' agreed Debra,
tidying her desk and gathering up her bag.

He walked with her to the main door. She was
apparently the last to leave. 'I trust you've enjoyed
your first day here,' he said as he locked up.

'Immensely,' smiled Debra. 'I wonder where Mr
Oliver went.'

Mr Fu shrugged. 'He comes and goes. We get
quite used to him disappearing without a word.
How do you like living in his villa? It is a very
beautiful place, don't you think?'

'Very,' agreed Debra, pressing the button for the
lift, 'but I don't intent staying there. Liz and I want
somewhere of our own. I don't suppose you could
help us find an apartment?'

He looked doubtful. 'Rooms are scarce, snapped
up almost before they become available. Mr
Oliver's villa is big—plenty of room—why do you

want to move? You will be happy there, I know.'
He clearly thought her mad for wanting to live
anywhere else.

'I feel we're imposing,' said Debra. 'Besides, I'm
sure Mr Oliver himself won't want to put us up for
too long. It must surely affect his private life.'

A smile lurked in the old man's eyes, as though
some secret thought amused him. But he was a true
diplomat and said, 'Mr Oliver would never turn
out a pretty woman.'

Not if she was co-operative, thought Debra. Fu
Ju Wen evidently did not know what sort of a relationship she and Vane Oliver held.

Out on the street they parted ways.

'*Tsoi kin*,' said Mr Fu.

'Goodbye,' repeated Debra. 'I'll see you in the
morning.'

It took but a few minutes to walk through the
still busy streets to the Peak Tram Terminal. As
she sat in the cable car being slowly borne upwards
in what was reputed to be the steepest funicular
railway in the world, absently watching the land
drop away below, Debra wondered what Liz had
been doing with herself all day.

A sense of guilt came over her as she realised
that this was the first time she had given the other
girl a thought. She had been so tied up in her work
that everything else had passed from her mind.

Now she could not wait to get back. Poor Liz
must be bored stiff!

A premonition which had lurked at the back of
her mind ever since she discovered Vane's absence
came flooding to the surface when she eventually
arrived at the villa and Lin Dai informed her that
both Mr Oliver and Miss Freeman were out.

'He came back about lunchtime,' said the young housekeeper, 'and they went out together.'

'You have no idea where?' asked Debra sharply, apprehension stabbing.

Lin Dai shook her head. 'I'm sorry, Miss Delaney, but he did say they would be back for dinner. Are you going to wait, or would you like me to get you something to eat now?'

'I'll wait,' said Debra tersely.

In her room she slowly stripped off her clothes and stood beneath the shower, her face serious. Liz was young and inexperienced, Vane Oliver had no right taking her out like this.

It suddenly became all the more imperative to find a place of their own. If this sort of thing was going to happen the sooner they were away the better.

Angrily she towelled herself dry and pulled on a pastel pink cotton dress, sleeveless and low-necked, following the rounded curves of her breasts before falling in soft gathers.

She had not heard them come back, but when she made her way into the drawing room they were there. Liz sitting with a glass of sherry in her hand, Vane was standing near the window, ostensibly looking out across the gardens, but Debra had the feeling he knew everything that was going on inside the room.

A deduction that proved correct when he turned. She had made no sound on entering, only some sixth sense could have told him that she was there.

'A glass of sherry before dinner?' he enquired blandly, insolent eyes sweeping over her so that she grew warm with embarrassment.

She shook her head. 'No, thanks, I don't drink,

neither does Liz,' looking disapprovingly at the younger girl.

Liz's eyes were overbright. 'One won't hurt,' she said defiantly.

To a person unaccustomed to drink one could do a great deal of harm, thought Debra bitterly. 'Mind you keep it to one, then,' she snapped, 'and why didn't you tell me you were going out with Mr Oliver this afternoon?'

Before Liz could answer Vane said, 'Because she didn't know.' He was busy refilling his glass from a whisky decanter that stood on a lacquered table. 'I thought it would be a nice surprise. Why, are you jealous?'

Debra's eyes flashed. 'Jealousy doesn't enter into it. You know why I disapprove, Mr Oliver, and I should like your promise that it won't happen again.'

'Debra!' protested Liz heatedly. 'We had a wonderful time. He took me to the Botanic Gardens. We went in the aviary and there was this toucan who seemed to take a fancy to me. You should have seen him clinging to the wire-netting and nibbling my finger. He didn't hurt, he was ever so friendly.'

But Debra had no interest in what Liz had to say, she was more concerned with the fact that they had been out together. Vane Oliver had no right to encourage the younger girl, especially after what she had told him about her having a crush on him. He was making matters worse.

She sat down heavily beside Liz on a sofa upholstered in a fabric featuring Oriental designs in pink, blue and beige. The pink matched the silk-covered walls which depicted scenes from Chinese folklore. The huge square of fringed carpet was mainly in beige and pink and the heavy silk curtains in the same blue as the upholstery.

It was a restful room, or would have been without Vane Oliver's presence. At the moment Debra felt it highly volatile—any minute the whole lot would go up in smoke.

'I'm waiting for your promise,' she said, looking directly at Vane, ignoring Liz's outburst.

'Then you'll have to wait a long time,' he said calmly, narrowed eyes coldly hostile. 'No one dictates to me.'

Meaning that if he wanted to take Liz out he would, regardless of what she, Debra, said or did. A cold fury filled her and she bounced out of the room, intending to have a word with Liz herself as soon as she got her on her own.

Outside she almost bumped into Lin Dai who had arrived to announce that dinner was ready. In the mood she was in Debra felt she could not face eating; only the thought that she would be throwing her friend and Vane Oliver together again made her join them in the dining room.

As she ate her way through the many courses that make up a Chinese meal Debra found herself being left out of the conversation, which did nothing to improve her temper. By the time they had finished and taken their coffee back into the drawing room she was ready to explode.

After a while she could stand it no longer and left them to it, going out into the gardens, which at any other time would have delighted her but which tonight left her cold.

She scarcely noticed the Chinese roses or viburnums, the exquisite azaleas, but walked aimlessly, ending beside the pool, sitting on the edge and trailing her fingers in the water.

A light footstep on the path disturbed her, and it was with a feeling of apprehension that she saw her employer approaching.

Without preamble he said, 'Liz is upset. What made you rush off like that?'

Debra looked at him stonily. 'I was in the way.'

'I doubt she would ever think that,' he returned steadily. 'She's been telling me how good you've been to her since her parents died.'

Pushing herself up, Debra said, 'She was heart-broken. I had hoped this change of environment would do her good.'

'It brings back memories of the years she spent here when her father worked with yours.'

She looked at him sharply. 'Not unhappy ones, I hope?'

He shook his head. 'On the contrary. She says she's beginning to feel at peace with herself.'

Was this simply because of her surroundings, or had this man something to do with it? wondered Debra. A brief frown flickered across her smooth forehead and she turned, staring down into the silver water, watching the golden carp slide gently between cream and purple water lilies.

'I'm glad,' she said quietly, but she was not sure she meant it. In accepting this job she had had no idea that Vane Oliver would become a part of their lives, and it troubled her.

She was naturally happy that Liz was recovering from her grief, but it was her relationship with this man that bothered her. She was quite sure he was simply amusing himself at her expense, no doubt getting a kick out of dating an innocent young girl instead of the sophisticates with whom he usually associated.

It appeared Vane Oliver also doubted the sincerity of her pleasure, because he caught her shoulder and spun her round. 'Are you really glad?' he demanded. 'Or are you jealous that I'm paying Liz more attention than you?'

'Take your hands off!' cried Debra, stepping back and glaring hostilely up into his handsome face. He was devastating, she realised with surprise. She had known he was a good-looking man, but she had never looked at him closely until now. No wonder Liz was smitten. Those thickly fringed eyes were enough to set any woman's heart fluttering— if she was stupid enough to let herself get involved.

Hardening her heart to such vagrant thoughts, Debra continued, 'And that's a ridiculous statement. Why should I be jealous? You know perfectly well how I feel about your attentions to Liz.'

His eyes gleamed derisively. 'I think you're lying, or trying to kid yourself. It's because I'm making a fuss of Liz that you walked out. You couldn't stand to see her receiving so much attention. Change your attitude and it could be you.'

Debra was furious. 'My God, Vane Oliver, you're the most conceited man I've ever met! I'm your employee and I know my place. I am not jealous of Liz, nor ever will be, it's what you're doing to her that worries me.'

'I haven't noticed her raising any objections.' The wide mouth quivered with undisguised humour. 'Don't you think you're making a fuss about nothing?'

'Not really,' she said tightly. 'Liz isn't old enough to know what she's doing. Besides, she's been through a big emotional trauma and she's very vulnerable. I wouldn't like to think she's heading towards more suffering.'

The beautiful deep-set eyes regarded her steadily. 'I think you misunderstand your young friend. She's perfectly capable of taking care of herself.'

'Not where men like you are concerned,' she snapped. 'She's had no experience.'

'And you have?' Mockery curved his lips, and she ought to have read the warning signals in his eyes.

But she was so incensed she carried on heedlessly, 'At least I know more about men than she does. If you want my opinion you should choose someone nearer your own age. Liz is a baby—she——'

'Like you, perhaps?' He was taunting her now and enjoying it, and Debra was becoming more irate by the second. Precisely when he began to advance she had no idea, and she was alarmed when she felt his hands behind her back, pulling her determinedly towards him.

'What are you doing?' she demanded angrily, pounding her fists ineffectively on his chest. He was all muscle, hard and sinewy, and filled with a magnetism that she had not suspected.

'Trying to prove, my little spitfire, that it's not only Liz I'm interested in.'

She opened her mouth to protest, only to find it possessed by a pair of cool demanding lips that quite clearly were not going to take no for an answer.

There was only one way to deal with a man like this, she decided, closing her eyes and quite deliberately remaining cool and aloof.

Vane was unfortunately a physically exciting man whom she found hard to resist, and it was impossible to check the sudden quickening of her pulses. She did her best to ignore their rapid beating, however, and stood quite rigid, assuring him that his attentions meant nothing.

It took a few minutes for him to realise that he was not getting anywhere, and then he held her from him, looking crossly into her eyes.

Before he could speak she said stiffly, 'Mr Oliver, you more or less forced me to come to Hong Kong, you installed me in your villa against my will, but I'm certainly not going to let you make love to me against my wishes!'

His silver eyes gleamed. 'Make love to you? Aren't you rather jumping to conclusions?'

She felt swift humiliation, but defiantly tilted her chin. 'I know what type of man you are, and I shall do everything in my power to stop Liz falling in love with you!'

His sigh was deep and impatient. 'So we're back to that again. Somehow I don't think your friend will thank you for interfering.'

Debra shrugged. 'I've no doubt she'll tell me to mind my own business.'

'Then why the hell don't you?' His voice was harsh and aggressive, and Debra felt a quiver of something approaching fear.

'Because I'm worried about her—I feel responsible.'

His laugh was unexpected. 'What a fierce little protector you are! But I fear you're wasting your energy. Liz is quite safe, you have no need for anxiety.'

He took her hand and led her towards the house. Debra saw the blind move, and wondered uncomfortably whether her friend had seen Vane kissing her. Was she really upset because she had walked out on them, or had Vane been making that up?

Feeling that perhaps now was not the best time to tackle Liz about her deepening friendship with Vane, Debra went to bed, but as she lay there she could not help wondering why Vane had made a pass.

Was it automatic with him? Did he attempt to kiss any girl in whose presence he found himself? Or did he really think she was jealous of Liz and had not wanted her to feel left out?

It was the obvious solution, yet not one to which she took kindly. It was not flattering to think that a man had kissed her from a sense of sympathy rather than because he found her attractive.

Not that she had wanted his kisses, she assured herself, but no girl likes to think she is an object of pity. It did nothing at all for her morale.

When Debra went down to breakfast the next morning Vane had already eaten, although he still sat on at the table. Of Liz there was no sign.

'Good morning, Debra,' he said. 'I trust you slept well?' and there was an odd gleam in his eyes that suggested he knew otherwise. Perhaps he thought his kiss had bothered her!

'Very well, thank you, Mr Oliver,' she managed brightly.

He wore a lightweight suit in palest blue. It sat perfectly on his wide shoulders, complemented his dark hair and tanned complexion. Begrudgingly she had to admit that he was the most attractive man she had ever met, and much to her disgust a faint quiver ran through her.

Picking up the heavy silver coffee pot, Vane filled her cup and pushed it towards her. 'Liz still asleep?' he enquired blandly.

'I presume so,' she said tightly. 'I haven't checked.'

It was unlike her not to look in on her friend, but somehow this morning she had felt reluctant to speak to Liz.

Liz was growing up too quickly. Almost overnight, it appeared, she had grown from a bewildered girl into a woman, and it was alarming, and Debra was not sure she knew how to cope.

It was at a time like this a girl needed her mother's guiding influence, yet, conversely, if her mother had not died none of this would have happened. She would still have been the same lovable child that she had always been.

Debra nibbled her toast and sipped her coffee, pretending not to notice Vane's impatience. It was strange, she was loath to face Liz, yet somehow she did not want to leave without speaking to her.

She prolonged breakfast as long as she could, hoping the other girl would put in an appearance, but at length was compelled to announce that she was ready.

'About time,' Vane growled. 'If you're going to take this long every morning we'd best make our separate ways—and how about Liz, hadn't you better say goodbye, or are you reluctant to face her after last night?'

So he too had seen the tell-tale movement of the blind! There was certainly not much that this man missed.

'Not in the least,' she lied defensively, 'but it would be a shame to disturb her if she's still asleep.'

'And how will you know without going in?' he enquired crossly. 'Really, Debra, you're acting very strangely this morning. If you hadn't told me differently I really would believe you were jealous of your young friend.'

Her brown eyes flashed. 'Jealous, because she fancies you? I'd be a fool! I have no interest in men.'

'Why?' he demanded abruptly. 'It's not natural.'

'It irks you, does it,' she demanded, 'that you can't get through to me like you do everyone else? What a pity! I'm a career girl first and foremost, and that's all there is to it.'

He spun her to face him. 'What if I say I don't believe you? What if I say that beneath that calm exterior you show the world I know there lurks a warm passionate woman?'

'You'd be deluding yourself,' she snapped, trying to pull free. 'And I'd thank you to keep your nose out of my private affairs. You're my boss, nothing more.'

Her reply angered him. His jaw tightened and a hardness with which she was becoming familiar glazed his eyes. 'Forgive me, I was forgetting. I'll get the car.'

As they turned Debra was shocked to see Liz standing in the doorway, a frozen expression on her face. How much of the scene had she witnessed?

'Liz,' she began, but was interrupted by Vane instantly throwing off his black mood and greeting Liz with a smile that held more than a hint of intimacy.

'Good morning, Lizzie, my sweet. We thought you were still asleep.' He covered the few yards between them, arms outstretched. 'I hope we didn't wake you.'

Mollified by his genuine pleasure, Liz allowed

herself to be drawn against him, glancing at Debra over his shoulder with triumph gleaming from her eyes.

Vane continued, 'I'm so sorry, sweetheart, we're just leaving. Will you be all right until we get back?' He pulled a wad of notes from his hip pocket. 'Here, go and buy yourself something nice, something pretty and feminine to cheer yourself up.'

Liz's lips brushed Vane's freshly shaven cheek. 'I'll be fine,' she said huskily. 'Thank you, Vane, you're so kind.'

'You can't accept it,' said Debra at once, face flushed with anger. 'Give it back this instant! Mr Oliver, what are you thinking of, giving Liz money like that? You have no right. She'll be perfectly happy playing records and reading, she has no need for new clothes.'

Liz pouted and looked as though she was about to burst into tears. Vane closed his hand over hers. 'You keep the money. Whether you spend it or not is up to you. Let's say it's a gift from you to me, a sort of thank you for giving up your home to come out here purely so that Debra could begin her new job. It was a very unselfish thing to do, and I appreciate it very much.'

He held her close a moment longer, his hands gently caressing. All Liz wore was a nylon nightdress and matching negligee, and Debra could tell that Vane was aware of every curve in her body, and Liz was using her new-found sexuality to its best advantage, pressing close, lifting her chin, lower lip quivering.

Debra was furious and clenched her fists and teeth in an attempt to stop herself from shouting her anger. Were there no limits to which this man would not go?

Gently now he put Liz from him. 'I'll see you later, my sweet. Be happy.'

Debra walked out without saying anything. What could she say except call Liz all kinds of a fool, and in the bemused state she was in it would make no difference.

But in the car she attacked Vane. 'How could you!' she cried. 'You're encouraging Liz, can't you see that? You're making things worse. Oh, God, I wish I'd never come here. I wish I'd never heard of you. I wish I'd never applied for that damn job!'

'You're getting all worked up over nothing,' he said calmly.

'Nothing?' she raged. 'You more or less molest Liz in front of me and you call that nothing? What are you trying to do, buy her friendship? You had no right giving her money. It's——' She searched for the right word and failed. 'Oh, I'm so annoyed I could scream!'

He slanted her a glance, face calm and unmoved. 'So why don't you? Go ahead, if it'll make you feel any better.'

'Oh!' She banged her fists on the dashboard. He was impossible! Nothing she said or did made any difference. She might just as well let them carry on in their own sweet way and say to hell with the consequences.

It did not improve matters when he sent for her shortly after she had settled into her office. Was this to be the normal procedure? she asked herself bitterly. Work was one thing, pleasure another, but never the two should mix.

She went along with misgivings, presenting herself before him rebelliously. 'Yes, Mr Oliver?' she said bitterly. 'You sent for me?'

He frowned at her insolence but passed it over. 'You haven't told me how you got on yesterday at Yam Ling Kee. Did you manage to sort out the problem?'

She got the impression he was hoping she had failed, and her chin firmed resolutely. 'It's all fixed. Mr Ho was most apologetic, but assured me he'll have a new lot ready by the required time. He did ask whether you would send the wrong consignment back.'

'It's on its way,' Vane replied tersely. 'I wish I was as convinced as you seem to me. We've had difficulties with them before. I hope that with you on the spot our troubles will be over.'

She glanced at him sharply. 'You can count on me, Mr Oliver. Of course, if you're not sure I've sorted things out satisfactorily you can go and see them yourself.'

The square jaw firmed, the grey eyes grew hard. 'Have I said anything to make you feel I can't trust you? If I hadn't thought you could do the job, Miss Delaney, I wouldn't have volunteered you for it.'

'Then why the doubt?' she flashed.

He sighed impatiently. 'Simply because it's a new job. You've not been trained for this sort of thing.'

'Common sense is all that's needed,' she snapped, 'and a knowledge of the trade, and I think I have that. We did have a very thorough training at the College of Art. I not only studied shoes and handbags, but dress design as well. The two go hand in hand, wouldn't you say?'

He shrugged. 'What else did you do with yourself yesterday? Mai Mai tells me you were very interested in the designs she's currently working on.'

Debra was surprised. Mai Mai must have been waiting for him as soon as he arrived. Somehow the thought of the two of them together hurt.

Vane and Mai Mai, Vane and Liz. Why was she so against his friendship with any other woman? It was not as though she fancied him herself. Having Vane Oliver for a boy-friend was the last thing she wanted.

'I did a few sketches,' she said, 'of belts and shoes that I thought would look good with them. Would you like to see?'

If she was hoping for encouragement she was disappointed. 'Later,' he said. 'I have other things to do first. On your way out tell Mai Mai I want her again, will you?'

Back in her office Debra looked at the drawings she had done yesterday and in a fit of pique tore them from the drawing board and ripped them into shreds. For a while after that she prowled about her room like a caged tiger and when she could stand it no longer left the building, telling Mr Fu that she was going to check on Yam Ling Kee again in case they were still experiencing difficulties.

But all was well. They had actually finished machining most of the dresses and the girls were at work with the hand embroidery over which all the fuss had been made.

Debra was amazed they had got on so quickly and wondered whether they had worked through the night to have made such progress. The room was filled with benches at which sat rows and rows of Cantonese girls, all busily embroidering dresses for Vane Oliver.

She felt guilty, almost as though it was her own fault that these girls had been caused this extra work, but Mr Ho was politeness itself, apologising once again for the mistake that was, he said, their own fault.

During the course of their conversation Debra discovered that the Yam Ling Kee Company worked exclusively for Vane Oliver. If they lost his business it meant they were out of work. Suddenly she understood why they were so anxious to please.

It was lunchtime when she had finished, and she went into one of the hundreds of restaurants Hong Kong boasted, enjoying mushroom and rice soup and Cantonese roast chicken.

It was after two when she got back, and only seconds after she had entered her office Vane came striding in.

'Where the devil have you been?' he demanded angrily. 'I wanted you. You had no right to go missing!'

Debra stared at him steadily. 'I told Mr Fu where I was going. If he didn't pass the message on then that's not my fault.'

'I got the message all right,' he continued belligerently. 'But why wasn't I told personally? Don't you think that I should be the one who has the say in where you go and what you do?'

Debra was astounded, but endeavoured to keep her temper. 'You were tied up with Mai Mai, I didn't want to disturb you.'

'Some excuse,' he snapped. 'We were not discussing anything so private that I could not have been interrupted.'

She must have looked disbelieving for he continued, 'My God, Debra, don't say you suspect me in that quarter as well? You seem to have a fixation about me associating with other women. I can assure you that my dealings with Mai Mai are strictly business. She's good at her job, I value her work, but that's all there is to it. Satisfied?'

'You don't have to explain,' she said tightly. 'It was just Mai Mai's attitude that made me think——' She broke off. 'Oh, well, it doesn't really matter. What I do object to is you going on at me about my job. If you wish me to ensure that your factories are carrying out the work correctly then you must allow me to visit them whenever I feel it necessary, without having to ask permission.'

His frown deepened. 'My dear Miss Delaney, just as soon as you're acquainted with the job you'll be given free rein. Until that time I want you to remain here unless I personally send you out.'

Infuriated by his arrogant manner, Debra said, 'You mean, if it's discovered that someone's made an awful mistake and you're out of the office I can't go along and correct it?'

'I mean nothing of the sort!' he yelled. 'You'd use your discretion. You know damn well what I mean, why be so awkward?'

Because you're being bloody-minded, she wanted to answer, but at that moment Mr Fu walked in, and no way could she offend the old gentleman by such unladylike remarks.

The two men left the office and Debra sat down limply. Arguing with Vane took everything out of her. She did not feel she had the energy to do anything else that afternoon.

Exactly why he had objected to her going out she could not imagine. It was not as though it was private business. Her lips tightened. If he was always going to be so unreasonable working here would be sheer purgatory.

She was glad Mr Fu had called him away. His dominant presence filled the room until it became overpowering. She felt stifled, despite the air-conditioning, and slid open the windows.

But Hong Kong's heat made no impression. If anything it was warmer still, and she flopped down again at her desk, looking forward to five o'clock and the welcome journey home. Up on the Peak it was cooler, at least ten degrees, and although humid, it was certainly fresher than down here.

She was just beginning to unwind when Vane came back, still in the same foul mood, and clearly quite prepared to do further battle.

'Where are those sketches you did yesterday?' He dropped into a chair on the other side of her desk, his hand held out in readiness.

Debra indicated the waste paper bin. 'In there,' she said bluntly. 'Would you like me to stick the pieces together for you? I'm sure there must be a reel of Sellotape around somewhere.'

'Don't be funny,' he snapped. 'What are they doing in there? Weren't you satisfed with them? From what you said this morning I thought you were pleased.' He studied her face for a few moments. 'No, don't tell me, I can guess. You were annoyed with me and tore them up in a fit of temper.'

Embarrassed that he had read her so clearly, Debra said defiantly, 'They weren't much good anyway. I'll do some more, if that's what you want.'

'I do,' he said peremptorily. 'It's a job I was

going to give you in any case. I was pleased to hear that you had the initiative to begin work on them yourself.'

Debra felt flattered and began to smile, until he continued:

'Pleased with my own judgment in selecting you from the numerous candidates who applied.' He rose and walked towards the door. 'Don't let me down, Debra. I'm going out now. I'll see you back at home this evening.'

Her thoughts immediately turned to Liz. 'You're going to the villa?'

He did not have to answer for her to know that her guess had been accurate.

'It's a long day for a girl to be on her own,' he excused himself.

'Then why don't you hurry and find that tutor you promised?' she demanded. 'Then she wouldn't have time to feel bored. Or you could bring her here, of course. I'm sure there must be some work she could do.'

He grinned derisively. 'your green eye's showing again, Debra. I think you need to watch yourself rather than me.'

Before she could answer he had closed the door. Jealousy indeed! It was concern for Liz's welfare that bothered her, and well he knew it. But how she was going to get through to him that he was doing more harm than good she had no idea.

Vane Oliver was a law unto himself. If he wanted to do anything he did it, regardless of whose feelings he trampled in the process.

CHAPTER FOUR

DEBRA was shattered when she arrived back at the villa to discover that Liz and Vane were out again. Things were moving at far too great a pace for her peace of mind.

She found it difficult to relax, only picking at the delicious dishes prepared by Vane Oliver's splendid cook. Later she walked in the garden, glancing frequently towards the gateway, wondering where they were, what they were doing, how long they would be.

Liz had no experience of men such as Vane; he could do irreparable harm. Oh, why had she ever allowed herself to be persuaded to come here? She should have stuck to her guns and remained in London. He had probably only been bluffing when he said she would not have the job of designer if she did not go to Hong Kong.

At eleven Debra was still on edge. Liz never stayed out this late. Had anything happened? Why hadn't they left a message as to where they had gone?

It was well past midnight when she heard his car. She was in the drawing room, in darkness. Now she got up and switched on a lamp, throwing the delicate room into shadows, disguising the loveliness of the silk-clad walls.

She picked up a magazine, sat in the circle of light and pretended to be reading, only looking up when the door was pushed open and

Liz burst in excitedly.

'Debra, you needn't have waited up.' She was vibrant and glowing, like someone in love, thought Debra painfully.

'I've not waited particularly,' she replied with an attempt at lightheartedness, not wishing to prick Liz's bubble of happiness in front of Vane. She could wait until she got her alone. The girl must be warned—if it was not too late. 'I was engrossed in a story, I hardly noticed the time.'

Vane, who had followed Liz into the room, plucked the book from her fingers. 'Clever girl, reading upside down.'

Debra shrugged selfconsciously. 'Okay, so I was waiting. Isn't it natural I should feel worried? I had no idea where you'd gone.'

'Liz is quite safe with me,' said Vane, as though it was obvious.

'Of course,' added the younger girl, clinging to his arm and gazing adoringly up into his eyes. 'We've been to the opera and then for a meal. I've had a wonderful time!'

Debra could hardly believe that. She knew what Chinese operas were about—gaudy costumes, elaborately made-up faces, and plenty of noise.

No, it was the man himself who was the attraction, and the more time they spent together the less Debra liked it. To him it was all a game, there was no way that he could fall for a slip of a girl like Liz. It was merely a way of passing the time, satisfying his craving for female company.

Women were his life. Women surrounded him. He designed clothes for them, they modelled for him, worked for him, and in between he wined and dined them, and undoubtedly made love to them.

But he was not going to make love to Liz, not if Debra had anything to do with it. She said tightly, 'I'm glad you've enjoyed yourself, Liz. I think it's time you went to bed now, though. You're not used to such late nights.'

Liz pouted and looked appealingly at Vane. He smiled ruefully and nodded. 'Debra's right—a pretty girl like you must have her beauty sleep.' He kissed the tip of her nose and pushed her gently away. 'Goodnight, sweetheart, pleasant dreams.'

She went then, reluctantly, but because Vane had insisted she did not argue as she would have done with Debra.

As soon as they were alone Debra turned on him. 'You had no right to take Liz out like that! Hasn't anything I've said made any difference?'

Amusement lurked in his dark eyes. 'Not a bit. How about a nightcap?'

'Don't change the subject,' she snapped, watching him angrily as he filled two glasses, handing one to her and swallowing the contents of the other as though badly in need of it.

She looked at him tightly. 'Are you trying to tell me that you'll take Liz out as often as you like, regardless of how I feel?'

He shrugged lazily, leaning back against the mantelpiece, eyes half hooded in that sensual way he had. 'But of course. Liz enjoys it, she's emerging from her grief. Why shouldn't I entertain her?'

'Why should you?' cried Debra. 'She's too young, for one thing. God, I never knew you were a cradle-snatcher!'

'I'm sure you've got it all wrong,' he said heavily. 'We're friends, that's all. I'm helping her readjust.'

'Is that what you call it?' tossed Debra scornfully. 'You're a fool if you think I'll believe that.' She did not care that she was talking to her employer—let him sack her if he liked, it might be for the best.

Unperturbed, he lifted his wide shoulders, saying evenly, 'Don't let your prejudice spoil you, Debra.'

She gasped. 'Can't you see what you're doing? Leave Liz alone, please, before it's too late.'

His eyes gleamed. 'Perhaps I should turn my attentions to you. Would that make you happier?'

She looked at him aghast, at the same time noticing the way his short dark hair followed the lines of his well shaped head, the hollows in his cheeks giving him a hungry look, as though he didn't bother too much about eating.

Unbidden came the thought of his kiss out there in the garden, and the quickening of her pulses told her that she was not as immune to him as she made out.

'It would revolt me,' she said desperately, in an endeavour to hide the true state of her feelings.

He stepped forward, a brief frown creasing his brow. 'Brave words, my little Debra. I've a notion to prove you're a liar.'

'You touch me and I'll——' She would what? Scream? What use would that do, except bring Liz flying back, and she had no desire to upset the other girl unnecessarily.

'I'm waiting,' he said softly. 'What would you do, I wonder? Kick, bite, struggle? Or would you decide that fighting was unladylike and take what was being offered? Who knows, you might even enjoy it.'

'Enjoy—kissing you?' Debra strove to sound

disdainful. 'When I let a man kiss me it's because I want him to.'

'I was not suggesting that I force my attentions,' he replied steadily, moving slowly nearer, his magnetic eyes holding her own so that she could not have moved had she wanted to.

She had never met anyone with quite such a dynamic personality. His virility was overpowering, sapping her strength, making her almost wish he would kiss her.

Slightly breathless, she said, 'There's no other way that I would let you touch me. I'm sorry, Vane, if I don't conform. It must come as something of a shock.' She had to keep talking, anything to take her mind off the hypnotic messages he was sending her.

It was easy to understand how Liz felt. Vane Oliver had an undeniable charm that no woman in her right mind could resist—and to someone as inexperienced as Liz he must seem like Prince Charming himself.

'Actually,' she continued, her voice shaky with suppressed emotion, 'you disgust me. You make no secret of your desires, and the fact that you've turned your attentions on an innocent girl like Liz makes it a thousand times worse.'

Anger replaced his amusement, deep dark anger that turned his face into stone. 'I'd be careful what I was saying if I were you, Debra.'

Apprehension tingled her awareness, but she lifted her chin determinedly. 'Does the truth hurt? Can't you take it? What's the matter, has no one ever told you what they think of you before? Perhaps they were all too frightened. But I'm not, I couldn't give a damn what you think, my main concern is for that young girl whose life you're corrupting, I——'

Her words were halted as he took her roughly by the shoulders and shook her so vigorously that her teeth rattled. 'That will do, Debra. I won't have any more of this, do you hear?'

'You can't stop me talking,' she blazed, more angry than ever. 'If you don't want to listen then go out of the room, because I'm far from finished. There's a whole lot more I want to tell you, things that should have been said a long time ago. It's about time somebody pricked your precious male ego, and I shall take great delight in doing it!'

He had stopped shaking her, but his hands still clamped her shoulders and she felt limp despite her brave talk. Her eyes, however, flashed fire as she lifted her head to see what effect her words were having.

The shock of his mouth on hers was like something she had never felt before. It was nothing compared to the kiss he had given her last night. Then he had been experimenting, testing her reaction, and had stopped when he got no response.

Now, though, he was taking her in anger, his lips bruising and punishing, assaulting her senses in a way that only he knew how. Almost involuntarily her lips parted beneath the pressure of his mouth.

There was something physically exciting about this kiss and there was no way that she could resist. Without her knowing it her arms snaked behind his head, holding him even closer, their passions fusing as one.

The virile strength of his body against her own aroused her, the hard lean length of thigh, muscled chest crushing her breasts, the intoxicating male smell of him. It was as though they were both hungry for each other, as though this coming together was something that they had both wanted for a long time. She was imprisoned against him, his hands moving with expertise over her body, and she strained even closer, wanting this moment to go on and on.

Punishment it might be, but never before had she felt such exquisite pleasure. She wanted Vane to hurt her, indeed enjoyed the pain as her lips were ground against her teeth.

He lifted his head momentarily to grate, 'Have you finished? Is there anything else you want to say? Because if so——'

She shook her head mutely, surprised to find her anger had disappeared.

Suspicion darkened his eyes and his mouth clamped on hers for another long second before he abruptly let her go. 'Now you know what to expect the next time. Let me give you a little advice— keep your opinions to yourself in future, or you might be sorry you ever opened your mouth!'

Debra dropped into a chair, wanting to speak, but she couldn't, and with a hand that trembled she picked up her drink.

The amber liquid did nothing to steady her jangled nerves, and to make matters worse Vane stood over her, watching, fully aware of the effect he had had on her.

His lips twisted mirthlessly. 'Think you can manage to drag yourself to bed, or would you like me to carry you?'

His sarcasm injected her with new life and she shot up. 'I can manage, thank you,' she said stiffly, and walked unsteadily towards the door, aware that his eyes were upon her all the time.

Quite how she opened it and walked through without her legs crumpling beneath her she did not know. But somehow she got to her room, closing the door thankfully behind her and switching on the light.

She wanted nothing more than to crawl into bed. He had somehow managed to drain every ounce of feeling from her, leaving her exhausted and a little ashamed. She ought to have struggled, denied him the satisfaction of meting out his punishment. God, what must he be thinking?

Her face flamed and she began to cross the room. It was only then that she saw Liz sitting on her bed, apparently waiting for her.

'What do you want?' she demanded crossly. Now was not the time for a confrontation with the other girl. In the morning would be soon enough, when she had had time to gather her senses. She felt too weak to think straight at the moment.

'What's the matter?' demanded Liz suddenly. 'What have you been doing? Look at your lips! Have you been kissing Vane?' Jealousy blazed in her blue eyes.

Glancing into the dressing table mirror, Debra was aghast to see her bruised and swollen mouth. But perhaps it was a blessing in disguise. 'He kissed me against my will,' she said tightly. 'That's the type of man he is, Liz. Perhaps now you'll realise that he's not the sort of person you ought to be associating with.'

'You m   have done something to make him do that,' cried the younger girl, jumping up from the bed to stand in front of Debra. 'Did you invite his attentions, did you provoke him? He wouldn't do that just for nothing.'

Debra shook her head and attempted to take Liz into her arms. 'No, no, it was nothing like that.'

But Liz shrugged away, a look of hatred on her face that Debra had never seen before. 'I know what your game is!' she yelled. 'You're trying to take him from me. You're jealous, jealous because he pays me more attention than you!'

'Liz, please——'

But the other girl would not be quietened. 'It won't work, you know. He loves me, he says I'm different from other girls. And he treats me with respect. He wouldn't do *that* to me,' indicating with disgust Debra's reddened lips.

At least that was something, thought Debra, but she did not like to hear that Vane loved Liz. 'Has he said he loves you?' she asked anxiously, her eyes searching Liz's face for the truth.

The blonde girl tossed her head lightly. 'Not in so many words, but he does, I can tell.'

'You can tell no such thing,' returned Debra harshly. 'He's kind to you because he feels sorry for you, but that's all. It's not love, nor ever will be—you're too young for the likes of Vane Oliver.'

'What are you trying to tell me?' queried Liz in a voice that shook. 'That he prefers someone like you?'

Debra shook her head passionately. 'Not in the least. I know I don't fall into his category—and he doesn't appeal to me either, in case you're wondering. He's my boss, full stop, and there's nothing between us, nor will there ever be.'

Slightly appeased, Liz said, 'Then why did he kiss you?'

'I goaded him into it,' explained Debra patiently. 'I was trying to tell him what I thought of him for encouraging a girl like you. I suppose I told him a few home truths and he didn't like it.'

'I still don't see why he kissed you,' persisted Liz with childlike curiosity.

'Men are funny creatures,' said Debra. 'They do strange things. It was his way of shutting me up.'

Liz looked hurt. 'Did you enjoy it?'

'Does it look as if I did?' Debra glanced again at her reflection, touching her lips experimentally with her fingertips. 'I like my men gentle, not like bulldozers.'

She gained the smile she had hoped for and this time the other girl let her gently gather her into her arms. 'Please be careful, Liz. Don't mistake Vane's kindness for anything else.'

But she knew that her words fell on deaf ears. Liz was completely smitten by Vane Oliver and would only learn the hard way that he did not return her feelings.

Debra was very unhappy when she climbed into bed a short time later. She did not want Liz hurt again, could not bear the thought of that haunted expression that had followed her parents' death coming back into her eyes. She was too young for such emotional traumas; she did not know how to cope with them. But like all young people she would not be told.

The fact that Debra herself was only five years older did not occur to her. She felt like a mother to Liz and in the same way wanted to protect her from the hard knocks of life.

The next morning Debra was almost afraid to face her employer. she had lain awake far into the night reliving their passionate embrace, mortified at her own reaction, wondering how she could possibly have enjoyed something that was intended as punishment.

Worst of all was the fact that Vane must have known how she felt. He was far too experienced not to know. Had he gloated over his victory? Would there be a self-satisfied smile on his face when they met?

Before going in to breakfast she popped her head round Liz's door and gave a smile when she saw the girl asleep, her blonde hair in charming disarray on the pillow, her lips curved happily. She looked as innocent as a babe—and that was all she was, thought Debra. God help Vane Oliver if he hurt her!

To her relief the breakfast room was empty. There was evidence that he had eaten, but of the man himself there was no sign. Debra had almost finished her toast when he came in, dressed for the office.

'Good morning, Debra are you ready?'

She gulped down her coffee and stood up. 'Quite ready, Mr Oliver.'

In one way it was a relief to see that he did not intend to carry on their battle of the previous evening, but on the other hand she had no desire to become too friendly. So far as she was concerned he was in the wrong, and nothing would make her change her mind.

It was difficult, in the close confines of his car, not to be aware of his physical attraction. There emanated from him an almost tangible sensuality and it took all her willpower to convince herself that he meant nothing to her.

His kiss last night had opened her eyes. there was an indefinable something that drew her to him, that must draw all women to him. She must push it from her mind, continually tell herself that he was a womaniser, that he flitted from woman to woman like a butterfly to a flower.

Besides, he had not kissed her because he felt attracted. He had been angry, and seen it as the only way to shut her up.

Even so there was a definite awareness on her part and she shuffled in her seat, edging as near to the door as possible.

When she glanced across at Vane he was smiling, as though knowing exactly what was going through her mind, and this angered her so that she clamped her lips tightly and stared straight ahead through the windscreen.

It did not take them long to reach the busy streets of Hong Kong's Central District, as Victoria is more commonly called, and here Vane's attention was taken by cyclists weaving in front, the slower moving rickshaws, and the many children who used the streets as their playground.

Just before they reached the office he said, 'Liz and I are going to one of the floating restaurants in Aberdeen tonight, would you like to come?'

Debra froze. 'Not particularly. I have no wish to play gooseberry, even if I don't approve of your association with my friend.'

He brought the car to a halt in front of the towering building, laying a detaining hand on her arm as she made to scramble out.

An uncontrollable shiver ran through her, annoying her. The power of this man was incredible.

'By joining Liz and me,' he said, 'you'll see for

yourself that we're no more than friends.'

She glanced at him icily. 'That's not what Liz thinks.'

He sighed deeply, impatiently. 'All the more reason for you to join us. Is it a date?'

He leaned forward and kissed her cheek, a kiss so fleeting it felt no more than the brush of a butterfly's wing, yet the turmoil it created was like nothing she had ever felt before.

He was a tough, virile man, fully aware of his sexual magnetism, and he was using it on her now. He cupped her chin in his hand, his thumb moving sensuously across her lips. 'Say you'll come.'

His voice was deep velvet and at that precise moment if he had asked her to jump into a lake she would have agreed.

Was this how it was with Liz? Had she no control over her senses when this man blatantly used his animal magnetism to get his own way?

She nodded briefly, unable to tear her eyes away from his face. He smiled, a warm smile that reached through to her heart, softening it, making her realise how easy it was to give in.

In the lift he stood unnecessarily close, making Debra even more uncomfortably aware of his fatal charm. She could be in danger of making a fool of herself, she realised worriedly, and wondered why Vane had suddenly changed his attitude.

Fu Ju Wen met them agitatedly at the door, wringing his hands, his lined face even more deeply furrowed than usual.

'*Yaw mi yeh see?*' asked Debra at once.

'There's trouble at Chung Yin,' he replied, 'you must get out there straight away.'

Debra interpreted, found out exactly where they

were situated, and Vane said swiftly, 'We'll both go.' He gripped her arm fiercely and ushered her back towards the lift. His face was set now.

She had to trot to keep up with his long strides. 'Do you often have difficulties like this?' she asked, as they rode smoothly back down to the ground floor.

'Too often for my liking,' he growled. 'You can see now why I need you, why you're so desperately important to me.'

It made her feel good, strangely enough, this compliment by her employer, made her all the more determined to make a success of her job.

Mr Fu had not told them the exact nature of the trouble and neither of them knew what to expect. Debra thought it might be a similar mistake to the one at Yam Ling Kee, and she guessed this was on Vane's mind too.

It came as a considerable surprise, therefore, when they reached the old building to find the entire workforce busy with mops and buckets.

The owner of the factory met them at the door. 'We've had a flood,' he said, throwing up his hands. 'All your fine material is ruined!'

Talking through Debra, Vane asked, 'How did it happen?'

A tap had been left on, the man admitted. 'When we arrived this morning we found this. I am very sorry, very sorry indeed.'

Moving through into the workshop, they discovered that the water had leaked from an upper floor, completely ruining whole rolls of silk and partly finished garments.

Vane's lean face was dark with anger. 'You stupid, incompetent fool!' he yelled. 'Doesn't anyone make a check before you lock up for the night?'

The Cantonese man looked guilty. 'Not for such as that. It's never happened before. I'm sure that we can soon catch up, if you let us have some more material.'

Vane's eyes blazed when Debra translated. 'Tell him he's lost my business,' he raged, 'the whole bloody lot, and I shall want paying for the material he's ruined through his damn stupid neglect!'

The owner pleaded for him to change his mind, but it was no use. In the mood Vane was in nothing anyone said would make any difference. Debra felt sorry for the little man, but agreed with her employer that the building should have been checked.

Storming outside a few minutes later, Vane was still in a filthy mood, and apart from several deep angry sighs he said nothing on the return trip.

Debra shut herself in her office and got busy with the sketches she had promised Vane. His mood just now had been frightening and she was glad she had not been on the receiving end.

Had the factory owner argued any longer she would not have been surprised had Vane resorted to blows, he had been so angry.

She could understand him, when the material was some of the most expensive and was being made into elegant evening gowns, but as before she felt a slight sympathy with the unfortunate man whose livelihood had been lost.

Her sketches finished, Debra was reluctant to take them in to Vane until he sent for her. Instead she asked Mr Fu if she could have a list of all the factories who worked for them. She spent the rest of the day putting them into some sort of order, with the intention of paying each one a courtesy visit as and when she had the time.

On the stroke of five Vane came into her office. 'Are you ready?' he asked tersely, and it was quite clear that his evil mood still lingered.

It did not augur well for their night out, thought Debra, gathering her bag and accompanying him from the room.

In his car he said, 'Fu Ju Wen tells me you've asked for a list of the factories.'

'That's right,' she said warily, feeling that he might be going to raise some objections, particularly as he himself had not instructed her. 'Once I have my car I thought I'd call on them, check that everything's going well, that they're interpreting your designs correctly.'

He seemed to visibly relax, much to her relief. 'Good girl, that's exactly what we need. Mr Fu's ordered your car, but delivery may take some days. The way things are at the moment I think you need to get on with it. Borrow my car tomorrow—no, I'll come with you.'

Debra would have preferred to go alone. She did not relish the thought of whole hours spent together. 'I've finished those designs,' she said, thinking that perhaps he might want to sit and study those instead.

'Good,' he replied. 'I'll have a look at them some time—unless of course you take it into your head to tear them up again?'

His good humour was returning, and Debra smiled selfconsciously. 'I'll try not to,' she said demurely.

Back at the villa she was concerned to find Liz in bed. She looked pale and quite unlike her usual self. 'Darling, what's the matter?'

'Nothing,' said Liz hostilely. 'Leave me alone.'

It became clear to Debra that Liz, left on her own all day, had been brooding over what had happened last night, had blown the incident up out of all proportion, and was now laying the blame on Debra's shoulders.

But she said nothing of her suspicions. 'I'll get you some aspirin,' she said. 'Have you eaten? Can I get you something?'

'I want to see Vane,' said Liz petulantly. 'Send him in to me.'

'You can't see him here,' cried Debra, horrified. 'if you need to talk to him so badly then get dressed and come into the drawing room. I won't disturb you.'

But Liz was adamant. She wanted Vane and she wanted him here in her bedroom.

In the end Debra did not have to send for him. He came himself to see what the commotion was about, expressing concern when he saw Liz in bed.

Against her better judgment Debra left them alone, hoping that Vane would know how to handle the girl without causing her any more emotional upset.

She guessed that they would no longer be going to eat out and she did not bother to wash or change. She sat in the drawing room, pondering over what was going on along the corridor, whether Liz really was ill. It was so unusual for her to take to her bed.

When eventually Vane put in an appearance she looked at him expectantly.

'Liz is settled now,' he said. 'Poor child, she has a mild dose of Hong Kong tummy. She's been ill all day, but she wouldn't let Lin Dai send for either of us.'

'Oh, I must go to her.' Debra was filled with remorse for even thinking that her friend might have been putting it on.

He shook his head. 'She's almost asleep. The doctor's been in and left a sleeping tablet for tonight. I shouldn't disturb her now, she'll probably feel much better tomorrow.'

'But why didn't she tell me she was feeling ill?' demanded Debra. 'She said it was nothing. Why did she lie?'

'Perhaps she didn't want to spoil your night out,' suggested Vane softly.

Debra was aghast. 'You're not suggesting that we still go, with Liz lying there? It's unthinkable!'

'She won't even realise we've gone,' he said, 'once the drug's taken effect. Go and get changed or it will be too late to go anywhere.'

'I can't,' she protested in anguish.

Silver eyes glinted. 'You can, even if I have to dress you myself and carry you out to the car.'

And he was quite capable of doing just that! Debra hurried to her room, calling in on Liz first, partially satisfied when she saw that she was indeed asleep.

She chose to wear a cream silk jersey dress that could almost have been one of Vane's own designs. The close-fitting bodice was delicately embroidered and the skirt clung to her slim hips before falling in a swirl of knife-edged pleats.

She felt a different person, and it was all she could do to meet his eyes as she re-entered the room.

He held out his hands and twirled her round,

inspecting her carefully. 'Stunning! Perfection itself.' His critical designer's eye looked her up and down. 'You've given me an idea. I shall design a range for the smaller woman, it's a corner of the market I've not yet touched. Perhaps with an Oriental influence.' He looked at the silk wallpaper with its Chinese figures, at the Coromandel screen with its herons in flight above beautiful foliage. 'The Chinese have something. I shall call it my Hong Kong collection.'

His enthusiasm was infectious and Debra could not help agreeing. 'It would be marvellous, Vane. I always have difficulty in finding dresses the right size. I even had to alter this one.'

'You've certainly made a good job of it,' he said admiringly. 'I could stand here all night looking at you, but if we want to eat we'd best get moving.'

Their drive took them out of the city and across the island, past huge resettlement blocks with lines of washing hung over balconies, past hill cemeteries and squalid shacks, into the fishing town of Aberdeen with its incredible clutter of junks and sampans and stilt houses.

Gaudy neon lights blazed from the floating restaurants with their several piers and curving roofs, and Debra laughingly let Vane take her hand as he helped her into a waiting sampan.

A grinning Cantonese woman in wide black cotton trousers and a matching black jacket ferried them across to the Sea Palace, one of Aberdeen's vast floating restaurants.

Light bulbs like pearl necklaces decked each pier, there was an air of festivity and cheerful vulgarity. Debra loved every moment of it and was glad they were alone, resolutely pushing Liz's illness to the back of her mind, knowing that Vane would not have insisted on them going out if her friend had been really ill.

While they waited to be served they admired the view from the restaurant windows. Junks glided slowly past, motors chugging, patched sails spread on the night breeze.

'I once heard that ninety-five per cent of Hong Kong's population lives on the water,' she remarked.

'I can well believe it,' he said. 'It's truly amazing. It's like a complete town out there.' The harbour was laden with junks and sampans strung with washing. It was a fascinating glimpse into how other people live.

'They even have junks coming round selling their wares so that they need never leave their boats unless they want to,' she continued. 'It's fascinating, don't you think?'

'Interesting,' he demurred, 'but their life style wouldn't suit me.'

Conversation stopped when their meal was served. They ate Peking duck, the skin, the most prized part, cut into thin slices, dipped in chilli sauce and then wrapped in wafer-thin pancakes.

Their table was loaded with an endless variety of dishes—crabmeat and sweetcorn soup, fried prawns and sweet and sour sauce, and a host of other equally exciting foods.

Vane tried a little of everything, insisted that Debra do the same, and they finished with large glasses of jasmine tea with huge black tealeaves and the odd jasmine bud floating in it.

Revolving fans on the gilded ceiling kept them

cool, young girls performed dances with long, whirling scarves, and then it was all over and they were driving along the coast, despite Debra's insistence that she wanted to go home and check on Liz.

Vane stopped at Repulse Bay, one of the most picturesque beaches on the island. A crescent of pale sand was backed by hills covered in green shrub, tall white hotel blocks that had not been there the last time Debra was in Hong Kong.

'I used to swim here when I was a little girl,' she said.

'We can swim now if you like,' he laughed, preparing to take off his jacket.

Debra put out a hand to stop him. 'One of these days,' she said, 'when I'm prepared for it.'

He caught her hand, pulling her against him. She felt the rapid stirrings of his heart, and her own echoed in response.

It was a magical moment with a full moon overhead, the special tang of the Orient teasing their nostrils, and the gentle whisper of the sea curling across the pale sand.

She had the feeling that if she was not careful she would be getting more than she had bargained for. 'It's a beautiful night,' she said lightly, attempting to twist away.

Guessing her intentions, he tightened his grip, both arms snaked behind her back and she was imprisoned.

'What are you playing at?' she enquired tremulously, almost as frightened of the feelings that were surging through her as she was of the man himself.

It was ridiculous that she should so easily

weaken, especially after last night. She ought to be fighting him, declaring her hatred—instead of which her legs trembled and her heart raced as though she had been running.

'My reward for taking you out,' he mocked. 'Don't say you didn't expect anything like this.'

He spoke blithely, but she suspected he was serious, and she guessed that this was his normal pattern of behaviour after taking a girl out. He had probably treated Liz in the same manner! An appalling thought, because how would the poor girl be able to refuse?

'No, I did not,' she said tightly. 'Take me home now, I must see how Liz is.'

'Scared?' he taunted. 'Don't you think any good of me at all?'

She wanted to say no. She wanted to shout it at the top of her voice, but something stopped her. Instead she said, 'I don't think anything. I don't know what to think. I've never met anyone quite like you before.'

'I know you haven't,' he said. 'It sticks out a mile. You think I'm playing around with Liz, you hate me for it, yet you can't help feeling a little attracted towards me yourself.'

Again Debra tried to tug free. 'Of all the conceited, arrogant pigs!' she cried. 'I'm no more attracted to you than——'

'You're missing all the fun,' he cut in. 'Why hold yourself back when there's a whole new exciting sexy world waiting to be explored?'

'You mean you'd like to make love to me,' exploded Debra furiously.

He nodded, suddenly serious. 'Yes, I would—you're the most fascinating woman I've met in a long time. But I haven't got that in mind right now.'

Debra shook her head angrily. 'You said you were after your reward. Why else did you stop here? We could have gone straight back to the villa if your intentions were as honourable as you claim.'

'We could have done,' he said softly, 'but it seemed a pity to waste such a beautiful night, and Repulse Bay is one of the nicest spots on the island.'

She could not dispute this, and seen by moonlight it was doubly attractive, but she did not trust this man, she did not trust herself, and it was for this reason she continued her battle. 'It is beautiful,' she agreed, 'but now we've seen it can we go?'

His eyes glinted in the silvery light. 'In good time, my little friend, there's no hurry.'

A pair of lovers walked by, arms entwined, feet kicking the soft sand, laughing, kissing, oblivious of the two still figures.

'An admirable example,' said Vane softly. He tilted her chin and kissed her, his lips moving gently, expertly, with none of the violence with which he had assailed her last night.

Debra felt her whole being set on fire, but resolutely stood mute. She had no intention of giving herself away again. If and when she allowed herself to become involved it would be with a man who loved her, not someone to whom the whole thing was an experiment, a game he was playing.

As he sensed her resistance the pressure of his mouth increased, her lips were forced apart as he furiously attacked her defences. There was no escaping, no matter how she struggled, and after a few minutes she found she did not want to.

Of their own volition her hands again crept behind his head, her fingers mingling in his short wiry hair. Emotions ran riot inside her and she knew she wanted this kiss to go on for ever.

When Vane's mouth left hers to trace its way across her face, kissing her cheeks, her eyes, her ears, she revelled in every second, her eyes closed, her head sunk back on her shoulders.

When he stopped she felt bereft and hardly without thinking lifted her face for a further kiss.

He smiled softly and obliged, and for a few long minutes Debra was lost in a new and wonderful world. His was the touch of an expert. He knew exactly what he was doing, and she had no notion to resist.

Finally he pushed her away. 'I think that's enough—for now. For a girl who didn't want to be made love to you certainly made a quick about turn.'

She said tightly, defensively, 'I expect you have no trouble in making anyone give in to you—sooner or later.'

'You little bitch!' he snarled. 'You make it sound as though I kissed you for the sheer fun of it!'

'Well, didn't you?' she cried. 'There's no other reason that I know of. You've got your own way with Liz and now you're trying me out.'

'If I weren't a gentleman,' he gritted, eyes blazing, 'I'd hit you!'

'A bit too near the truth, am I?' Debra goaded.

'Shut up, damn you!' he muttered, gripping her shoulders and shaking her violently.

'Let me go!' she shouted. 'Never put your hands on me again, Vane Oliver—you've had all you're ever likely to get from me!'

The fact that his kisses had thrilled her made her all the more angry. She had weakened, allowed herself to be swayed by this man, and because there could be no future in it, it had to stop, right now.

She was quivering passionately and when he abruptly let her go she fell on to the sand.

Without even sparing her another glance he strode back to his car. She heard the engine start and then his voice roar into the darkness. 'If you're not in this car within ten seconds I'm going without you.'

Her first thoughts were to remain where she was, but they were a long way from home. Reluctantly she climbed in beside him, sitting stiff in her seat, clinging to the edge as he drove furiously back to the villa.

CHAPTER FIVE

VANE left for the office without Debra the next morning. In fact he had gone when she went in to breakfast.

She had spent a restless night worrying about their argument, knowing she had spoilt their evening, but deciding that he deserved it with his despicable behaviour.

Worrying too about Liz. She wanted to stay at home and look after her, but Lin Dai assured her there was nothing she could do, and wouldn't Mr Oliver be annoyed if she did not go?

Debra could not dispute this, but it was with reluctance that she left the sleeping girl to catch the railway car.

The top of the Peak was shrouded in mist, as it so often was, and the cool morning air made her head feel clearer, so that by the time she reached her destination things did not look so black as they had on first waking.

It was not until she walked into the office that she remembered Vane was supposed to accompany her today on her round of visits.

Her spirits sank. If he was still in the same black mood it would be a far from pleasant experience.

It was gratifying therefore when Mr Fu informed her that Vane had left his car at her disposal, he himself having gone to mainland Kowloon on the Mass Transit Railway.

This underground railway system was a new

innovation, and having heard of it Debra was keen
to try it for herself. Perversely she wished she could
have gone with him, consoling herself with the fact
that there would be another time.

His big car took some getting used to, and by
the end of the day Debra was exhausted. All the
factories she visited appeared to be doing the work
quite satisfactorily, and she looked forward to re-
porting to Vane that all was well.

But when she got home he still had not returned.
Liz was up, though, still looking pale and shaky,
but assuring Debra that she felt much better.

'Why didn't you tell me you were ill?' she scolded
gently.

The girl shrugged and said nothing, and Debra
decided not to press the matter. Liz obviously had
her own reasons for remaining silent.

The two of them spent a quiet evening reading
and listening to records, Liz constantly asking
when Vane would be back, and Debra unable to
answer.

She was relieved in one way that he was out. It
had been a long time since she and Liz had spent
any time together, though they were not as matey
as they had been.

There was only one person to blame for that,
thought Debra, and her heart hardened.

The next day was Saturday, but from force of
habit Debra rose early and was eating her breakfast
when Vane came into the room.

He had washed and shaved, but wore nothing
more than a short crimson silk dressing gown, his
feet pushed into leather-thonged mules. He greeted
her warmly enough, even though they had parted
in anger two nights ago.

'Good morning, Debra. You're an early bird, considering you don't have to go to work.'

'I was awake,' she said crisply, 'what point was there in staying in bed?'

'Some people do,' he replied, joining her at the table. 'I'm glad Liz is better. I just looked in, she's almost her normal self.'

His nearness disturbed her, made her speak more sharply than she intended. 'I wish you wouldn't go to her room.'

He frowned, helped himself to coffee. 'She's not complained, and she has been ill—I'm not completely heartless.'

Debra raised her fine brows. 'I don't suppose she would.' Accidentally his bare leg touched hers beneath the table, and it was as though a charge of electricity ran through her. She shot back in her seat, staring at him with wide shocked eyes.

'Now what?' he rasped angrily. 'I've not seduced her, if that's what's on your mind. I find her excellent company, very entertaining—more than can be said for her friend.'

'I'm sorry if you consider me a boor,' she said distantly, 'but you know the reason why.'

'I sure do,' he replied wearily, 'and I'm sick and fed up hearing the same old story. When are you going to get over your prejudice?'

She glared hostilely, wishing he wore something more civilised. Glimpsing his bare chest did nothing to stabilise her emotions. Her quickened pulses told their own story—she was relieved he had no way of knowing what was going on inside her. The cold front she projected was sufficient, she hoped, to convince him that they would never see eye to eye.

'When are you going to stop playing around with Liz?' she demanded. 'How do you think she's going to feel when you finally reject her?'

'As though it's the end of the world,' he jeered. 'Isn't that what you're thinking? I shan't walk out of her life completely, Debra, credit me with more chivalry than that.'

She sniffed sceptically. 'So long as I stay in this job, I suppose. What happens if I leave?'

Vane's eyes narrowed. 'Are you thinking of it?' and his voice came sharp and jerky.

'I could be,' she said slowly. In actual fact the thought had never entered her mind, but it interested her to see his reaction.

'Why?' he snapped, then, 'I'll raise your salary.'

She smiled politely, coolly. 'I'm perfectly happy with what I'm getting, Mr Oliver. It's just you I'm not happy about.' She held her breath, expecting an explosion. He would never let her get away with such rudeness.

His jaw tightened and a pulse jerked. 'You deserve a damned good hiding!' he grated, silver eyes like chips of ice. 'If you weren't important to the smooth running of my business I'd throw you out. My God, didn't your mother teach you any manners?'

'I seem to forget them when you're around,' she spat. 'You rub me up the wrong way.'

'What the hell do you think you do to me?' he fired back. 'A man can take so much, Debra, and I'm getting dangerously near the edge.'

The fierce look in his eyes thrilled her, she found a contrary delight in their verbal warfare. She tilted her chin slightly. 'You know what you can do about that, Mr Oliver.'

'Leave Liz alone,' he said doggedly, roughly. 'Hell's bells, you're like a record with the needle stuck. Can't you get it through your thick skull that she's quite safe? I have no ulterior motives. She won't suffer as a consequence of my friendship.'

He kept telling her that, but it was difficult to accept. If only he would leave Liz alone altogether—but to ask that was like waving a red rag at a bull.

Their eyes met and held, a magnetic attraction despite their antagonism. Debra was the first to look away. She pushed back her chair. 'I'll go and see Liz, if it's all right with you, if you haven't any prior claim on her attention.'

Her sarcasm was not lost on him. He shot up from the table and caught her arm roughly. 'I know you told me never to touch you again, Debra, but you've asked for it!'

She thought he was going to strike her, was totally unprepared when his mouth fastened on hers in yet another brutally punishing kiss, another bruising, vindictive assault which left her breathless.

When he threw her from him with a thick, 'Get out of my sight!' she fled the room gladly. Damn the man! What right had he to do this? She would not stay in his house a moment longer and put up with his total disregard for her feelings.

Without stopping to give the matter any further thought she burst into Liz's room. 'Get packed,' she ordered, 'we're leaving!'

Liz looked at her with wide startled eyes, pushing herself up in bed. 'What are you talking about—leaving? What's happened?'

'Because I refuse to live with that man any

longer, he has no regard for my feelings. He thinks he can do just what the hell he likes!'

'I'm sure you're exaggerating,' said Liz. 'He's always the perfect gentleman when he's with me. I can't see why he should treat you any differently.'

'You don't know the half,' snapped Debra. 'Get out of bed and start packing. I refuse to remain here a minute longer to be insulted!'

Liz's lower lip quivered. 'Must we go, Debra? I don't think I feel up to it. Besides, I'm so happy here. If we go back to England I shall be all upset again, I know I will.' Her big blue tear-filled eyes pleaded with her friend. 'Don't let a silly misunderstanding make you give up your job.'

'It wasn't silly,' choked Debra. 'We were discussing you, if you must know. I've tried telling him to keep his hands off, but it's no use, so it's best we leave before things get out of hand.' She pushed to the back of her mind all thoughts of Liz's illness. She simply had to get away.

'I won't go!' Liz wailed, throwing back the sheets and scrambling out of bed. 'You leave if you want to, but I'm not, I'm staying here with Vane.'

'Not by yourself you're not!' yelled Debra. 'The man's not to be trusted. He's using you, can't you see that? You're attractive, you're a novelty. It doesn't mean a thing to him.'

'You keep saying that,' cried the younger girl, tears running down her cheeks. 'But it's not true, none of it. Vane loves me and I love him, and I expect it will be only a matter of time before he asks me to marry him.'

Debra heaved a sigh, containing her temper with difficulty, reminding herself that Liz had been ill, and quite possibly did not know what she was saying.

'Liz, listen to me. Vane will never marry you. You're far too young, for one thing, and for another I'm quite sure he doesn't love you. It's all in your mind. You're making a big mistake. Please come back with me before it's too late.'

Liz shook her head positively. 'No, I refuse, and you can't make me.'

And Debra knew that with Liz in this mood there would be no moving her. One thing was for certain, she couldn't go and leave Liz here to the mercy of *that* man. All she could do was remain and keep her eye on her young friend and hope and pray she would get over her silly infatuation before too long.

She was convinced it was infatuation. Liz was not old enough to know her own mind. Vane was the first man she had been out with. It had been wrong of her parents to protect her as they had, but it was too late to do anything about that now.

'Very well,' she said reluctantly, 'we'll stay, but only on condition that you don't see so much of Vane.'

Liz nodded sullenly, but it was not a promise. Debra had not really expected she would give one.

'Do you feel up to going shopping, just the two of us?' she continued. 'The fresh air will do you good, it seems ages since we spent any time together.'

She waited until the other girl was ready, and was considerably annoyed when she found Vane still in the breakfast room.

He had dressed and the loose knitted cotton top clung to his muscular chest and shoulders, short

sleeves revealing powerful arms. Perhaps as well he
had chosen to punish her the way he had, thought
Debra. She would not fancy her chances if he used
physical strength.

He gave her a cool look but greeted Liz with a
smile that Debra could only describe as intimate.
'Ah, the invalid arises, and looking completely re-
covered, if I may say so.'

Liz kissed his cheek warmly. 'Still a little weak,
but otherwise better, thank you.' She sat down and
helped herself to coffee. 'Debra and I are going
shopping.'

'Good idea,' he nodded. 'I'll come too.'

Debra wanted to shout, 'No!' but already Liz
was smiling happily. 'Oh, goodie, we'll need a man
to carry our parcels.'

Debra fumed silently as Liz finished her meal,
racking her brains trying to find a reason to put
Vane off. But none came, and a short while later
they all three piled into his car.

At any other time Debra would have enjoyed
shopping in Hong Kong. She loved pushing
through the crowds, the air of feverish gaiety, the
bargaining which almost inevitably took place. But
today she could whip up no enthusiasm, not with
Vane holding Liz's elbow, courteous, attentive;
only Debra he ignored.

This was supposed to have been her day out with
Liz, she raged. He had spoilt it by joining them,
had made Debra feel as though she was the in-
truder, not he.

When he bought Liz a beautifully carved ivory
flower boat, a work of art created by the finest
craftsmen, she was angry enough to have smashed
it to pieces. When he asked if there was anything

she would like herself she shook her head savagely. 'I wouldn't take anything from you.'

His grim lips told their own story and she trailed miserably behind them as they moved from shop to shop, from market stall to market stall. She would have given anything to slip away unnoticed: her fear of leaving the two of them together was the only thing that stopped her.

When finally they stopped at one of the better class dress shops Liz urged her to try on a *cheong-sam*.

Debra shook her head. 'It would look ridiculous.'

'No, it wouldn't,' argued Liz. 'You're so tiny, it will be perfect. Oh, please, do try one. I wish I had your figure, I'd soon be in there.'

Vane, half smiling now, eyed her insolently. 'I too should be interested to see what it looks like.'

Reluctantly she agreed. The politely smiling assistant showed her into a dressing room where Debra slid out of her own dress and carefully into the silken *cheongsam*: It fitted her like a second skin, and despite her initial protests it was immediately apparent, even to her own prejudiced eyes, that it suited her. The tightly fitted stand-up collar emphasised her slim throat, the proud tilt of her head. The rest of the dress followed her curves devotedly, parting in slits on either thigh, revealing her slender legs, elegant in their high-heeled sandals.

Brilliant peonies flamed over the pastel silk of the dress—the Chinese wedding flower, thought Debra, and hoped Vane was not aware of its meaning.

When she appeared before them he pursed his lips in a soundless whistle, eyes approving, not missing one inch of her delicately rounded curves.

Liz was more open with her enthusiasm. 'Debra, it's perfect, I knew it would be. You look ravishing!'

Vane insisted she walk up and down in front of them, watching her with a critical eye. 'Will you help model my new collection?' he asked suddenly, surprisingly.

Without being given time to think Debra found herself nodding shyly, and then, embarrassed, ran back to the changing room.

She had never thought of herself as a model, tiny girls rarely stood a chance, but with his new ideas for the smaller woman, it was an exhilarating thought.

When she came out she discovered that Vane had already paid for the dress, absolutely refusing to take anything from her.

'I shan't wear it,' she said heatedly.

'Oh, but you will.' His eyes were alight with sardonic humour. 'You will wear it for dinner tonight—I insist.'

Try arguing with that, she told herself. His tone brooked no refusal and she felt too tired to put up any resistance.

She was glad when they were home. Vane disappeared and she and Liz lay outside on the loungers, her friend totally exhausted after all the walking they had done.

Here was peace, thought Debra. The teeming streets could be forgotten, even Vane Oliver faded from her mind. Thrushes sang in the eaves, dragonflies skimmed the surface of the pool, the golden carp swam lazily in the sun-dappled waters.

Debra dozed and when she awoke Liz had disappeared and Vane was lying in her place. Her first thoughts were to run away, but he appeared to be asleep, so she propped herself up on one elbow and studied him.

In repose his face was less lined, although the hollows in his cheeks were still there. He looked strangely vulnerable and she felt an urge to touch him, to trace the outline of that strong jaw and wide forehead.

He had stripped off his shirt and his broad chest was as tanned as his face, thinly covered with dark hairs, muscular and powerful.

With great daring she reached out and laid her fingers on his chest, felt the deep rhythmical breathing, the warmth and firmness of his skin.

When his hand shot up and imprisoned her own she was startled and attempted to pull away, her brown eyes wide.

'I'm sorry,' she husked. 'I thought you were asleep.'

'I realise that.' There was amusement in his face. 'Why did you touch me? To make sure I was real?'

'I don't know why,' confessed Debra. 'I did it without thinking.'

He smiled suggestively. 'Physical attraction?'

But this she would not admit. She shook her head positively. 'No, nothing like that.'

'An emphatic denial,' he jeered, 'often used to hide the truth. Tell me, little Debra, are you still thinking of leaving? Liz told me earlier that you were on the point of walking out.'

She looked at him coldly. 'What did you expect? You have Liz to thank that we're still here. If it hadn't been for her insistence we'd have been on a flight to London by now.'

He lifted her hand and pressed a kiss into the palm. 'Lovely, hot-headed little Debra! I wish you weren't so much against me, ours could be a beautiful relationship.'

'Like the one you have with my friend,' she whipped. 'Like the ones you have with all your girl-friends. Please remember that I'm your employee, nothing more, nor will I ever be.'

He dropped her hand and she thought he looked disappointed, but she knew she must be mistaken.

Pushing herself up, she marched away, sighing deeply. Was it always to be like this—one verbal battle after another? Would he never give up? Was it an obsession with him to have all women bowing at his feet?

As she dressed for dinner later Debra's heart felt heavy and she could whip up no enthusiasm. Liz had been in earlier, completely refreshed and bubbling over with high spirits, asking her opinion on which dress she should wear. They had decided on a sky blue silk which complemented her blonde hair and matched her eyes to perfection.

In honour of the occasion Vane wore a cream evening jacket over a brown frilled shirt. Debra's pulses raced when she saw him and for one mad moment wished it were only the two of them.

He smiled warmly as they came towards him in the drawing room, reaching out and taking a hand of each. 'You must be the two most beautiful women in the world. I consider myself honoured.'

Liz dimpled and kissed his cheek. 'Thank you, Vane. You look pretty devastating yourself.'

He offered his other cheek to Debra, frowning in annoyance when she deliberately turned away, looking at Liz and shrugging, as if to say, 'What do we do with someone like her?'

Crossing to the lacquered table, he poured three glasses of sherry. Liz accepted eagerly. Debra hesitated, took heed of the warning in his eyes, and received her glass. It was less than half full, and to have issued a definite refusal would have been like declaring open warfare.

She appreciated he was doing his best to be nice, to make this a pleasant evening for all three of them, but to her way of thinking it was farcical dressing up like this when there was no other company but themselves.

She felt that she was being made to look a fool in her *cheongsam* and resented it, and her expression reflected her disgruntlement.

The fact that Vane and Liz were able to talk freely did not help matters, and by the time they had finished their drinks and made their way to the dining room, Debra was feeling decidedly bad-tempered.

She sat down at the table, picking at her avocado, toying with the excellent seafood, stubbornly refusing to look at the others or join in their conversation, even though several times Liz attempted to draw some response.

When she heard Vane say, 'It's a shame she spoils her face with angry expressions,' her head flicked up sharply.

He was grinning and she knew he had intended her to hear. 'I don't find it funny,' she said coldly.

'Nor do I find your behaviour funny,' he returned, his smile fading. 'You complain when Liz and I leave you on your own, yet you're doing nothing to make this evening a success. Do you enjoy sulking?'

'I'm not,' she shot back.

'You could have fooled me.' His eyes were icy now, the humour gone.

'After you've bought her that beautiful dress as well.' Liz added her complaint to Vane's.

Debra threw her a vicious look. 'I didn't ask him to, he can have the damn thing back if by wearing it I have to put on a false front.'

'No one's asking you to be false,' hissed Vane. 'But a little co-operation won't hurt.'

With both of them against her Debra felt like running. How she sat there and pretended nothing was the matter she did not know. Only by a supreme effort did she manage to eat and talk and drink and try to look as though she was enjoying herself. But all the time she was aware of the close intimacy between Liz and Vane, and the more she saw the less she liked it.

When they had finished eating they took their coffee into one of the lesser used lounges, coolly decorated in shades of blue and grey. It reflected her mood, she thought, settling down into an easy chair in one corner, prepared to sit there for the rest of the evening.

Vane put on a record and invited Liz to dance, and the way her friend clung, the way she pressed her body close to his, made Debra ashamed. She wanted to snatch the girl away, tell her to stop making a fool of herself.

When the music ended and he asked her for the next dance it was all she could do to make herself walk into his arms. But soon the feel of his body against hers set her nerves tingling, increasing her awareness, and she wondered whether after all he could be right, and she was jealous of his association with Liz.

She dismissed the thought as nonsense, but as soon as the record finished she pulled away and ran from the room. She had had as much as she could stand for one day.

She had not anticipated that he would follow, had thought his dance with her had been a duty one and that he would spend the rest of the evening with Liz.

It came as a shock, therefore, when he caught up with her outside. 'Don't be an idiot,' he said tersely. 'Can't you see that you're spoiling the evening by your stupid, childish behaviour?'

Debra wrenched her arm free. 'I'm not a child!' she cried angrily.

'Then for God's sake stop behaving like one,' he snapped. 'Come back, or I really will have grounds to believe that you're jealous of me and Liz.'

'As if you'd care whether I'm there or not,' she cried. 'But I will come back, if only to keep an eye on you two. But don't ask me to dance again, because I won't.'

His eyes narrowed. 'Why, because you're afraid of the emotions I arouse? Do your wanton feelings shock you?'

His words shocked her. How did he know? Was she so transparent? 'I'm sure I don't know what you're talking about,' she said distantly.

A smile flickered briefly. 'You're only fooling yourself, Debra. I can read you like a book. Bear that in mind in future when you try to lie to me.'

'I don't lie,' she began, but he put a finger to her lips.

'Hush now, the battle's over. Life's too short to be spent arguing.'

It was almost midnight when Liz said, 'I'm tired, I'm going to bed. Thank you for a wonderful evening, Vane.'

She lifted her face to his and he kissed her warmly, holding her close, as though reluctant to let her go.

'I'm coming too,' stated Debra, moving towards the door. 'Goodnight, Vane.'

He released Liz and said, 'I'd like a word with you, Debra, alone.'

She looked at her friend, expecting to see opposition, jealousy. And it was there. The other girl threw her a venomous look before flouncing out of the room and banging the door behind her.

Things were getting out of hand, thought Debra. They ought to have left the country when she said she was going, instead of letting Liz persuade her otherwise.

Her young friend was becoming more deeply involved with each passing hour, and when the inevitable break came she would be heartbroken.

She glanced impatiently at Vane. 'What is it that can't wait until morning? I'm tired too. I have no wish to stay up and continue our argument.'

'Who says we're going to argue?' he asked mildly.

'Don't we always,' she said irritably. So far as she was concerned the last few hours had been far from pleasant. It had been sheer agony to see him and her friend dancing, and to have the evening prolonged now, especially when she could think of nothing he could possibly want to talk about, was the last straw.

'Sit down,' he commanded, pouring a drink and putting it into her hand. She had already drunk more tonight than she had in her whole life, but she took it with ill grace, staring moodily into the glass, waiting for him to speak.

When the silence lengthened she looked up to find him eyeing her thoughtfully. 'I can't even begin to understand you,' he said.

'Then why bother?' she returned. 'Accept me for what I am. Surely on a working relationship there's no need for us to—*understand* one another.'

Vane's eyes narrowed. 'You're right, of course, there isn't. I keep forgetting that you're an employee. I had hoped we would be friends.' There was a sudden withdrawal which she failed to understand.

'It's Liz who's your friend,' she said distantly.

'Yes—yes, it is,' he affirmed. 'Goodnight, Debra, you can go now.'

She was confused. 'I thought you wanted me for something.'

'I've changed my mind,' he said abruptly.

Swallowing her drink, spluttering as it went down the wrong way, she left the room gladly, puzzled over his sudden change, but not really caring.

She was tired, but not tired enough to fall asleep straight away, and when she heard Vane's footsteps outside a few minutes later, she was instantly wide awake.

Fully alert now, she listened, heard a tap on Liz's door, then it opening and closing, and soft muted voices, and then silence.

It could only mean one thing. Why else did a man go to a woman's room in the middle of the night?

Cold with fear now, Debra sat bolt upright, her

ears strained, listening. It was a long, long time before she heard him come out again.

She felt shocked, and angry, and sick, and perturbed—*and jealous!*

The shock hit her like a blow. She *was* jealous, she really was. And the reason—the reason why she had been so against his relationship with Liz became suddenly very clear.

She was in love with Vane herself!

The realisation left Debra stunned. It was something which had simply never occurred to her. She had been convinced that her dislike of his association with Liz was because she was concerned for her friend's virtue.

Perhaps it had been, in the beginning, perhaps it still was to a certain degree. She was convinced that his intentions were not serious, though.

He was thirty-six, still a bachelor, could have his choice of any woman with whom he came into contact—and they were considerable in his profession—so why pick a child like Liz?

It was her guess that he was amusing himself and her friend was going to fall hard, unless it was stopped right now before it went any further. It could be too late, of course. His going to Liz's room tonight told its own story.

As Liz would not listen to reason there was only one other solution—and that was to attract Vane to herself. It was a risk and a gamble, she could get hurt in the process, but if it would save Liz more heartache it would be worth it.

The plan appealed to her, loving Vane as she did, and she had no doubt that he would be a willing, if unsuspecting, partner.

She did not want a mere affair, though, she

wanted him to fall in love, the deeper the better, and then she would drop him like a red-hot brick.

It was dawn when she finally fell asleep and to her disgust almost midday when she awoke. Lin Dai informed her that Miss Freeman and Mr Oliver had driven over to Repulse Bay for an hour's swimming before lunch.

Sick with jealousy, Debra paced the house like a caged animal, listening for the sound of his car, angry with herself for caring but unable to do anything about it.

It was almost five when they finally returned. They both looked happy, but Liz's face held a slightly guarded expression and Debra guessed she was wondering whether she knew about their clandestine midnight meeting.

Endeavouring to hide her true feelings, Debra smiled. 'Had a good day, you two? You certainly look as though you have.'

Liz smiled guiltily. 'We were going to ask you to come with us, but you were so sound asleep I said it would be a shame to wake you.'

Debra was not sure she believed this. 'I'm surprised you woke so early yourself,' she said, 'after your late night.' She put deliberate emphasis on the 'late', and was disappointed when she got no reaction from either of them.

'I'm going to have a rest before dinner,' said Liz. 'I'm not as fit as I thought I was. That Hong Kong tummy sure takes it out of you.'

'And Debra and I will have tea on the verandah,' said Vane. 'You can tell me what you've been doing with yourself today.'

Going nuts, she could have said, but she smiled weakly and followed him outside.

Lin Dai brought their tea in delicate china cups decorated with red and gold dragons, and a plate of tiny rice cakes, which Vane ate with relish. Debra did not feel like eating, the mere thought of food choked her.

When Vane pursued his interest in what she had been doing, Debra said caustically, 'Nothing. What could I do on my own?'

Thick brows rose mockingly. 'Sounds like you're peeved because we went out without you.'

Debra sipped her tea, but silent for a moment or two. 'Because Liz went out,' she said at length, 'that's all. I had hoped to spend some time with her this weekend. I hardly see her when I'm working.'

'Because I take her out most nights?' he questioned deliberately, eyes watchful. 'I hope you're not trying to tell me that I should take you as well. There's a subtle difference in our relationship.'

His insinuation hurt, as he had meant it to, but as only last night she had reminded him that they were nothing more than boss and employee she could not very well dispute his statement now. 'I meant nothing of the sort,' she said tightly.

'Good,' he replied coldly. 'I'm glad that's sorted out. In case I forget myself in future perhaps you'll remind me.'

Debra eyed him guardedly, not sure whether he was mocking. With Vane in this frame of mind it was certainly going to be difficult to put her plan into action. She would have to wait until he was in a more mellow mood.

He finished the cakes and drank his tea, refusing a second cup. Sitting back, he closed his eyes.

'You don't have to stay with me,' she said

bitterly, when she could stand his silent presence no longer. 'I'm quite sure there must be something you'd rather be doing.'

At first she thought he was not going to answer, or he could have fallen asleep in the warm sunshine. Then she realised he was watching her from beneath lowered lids. 'There is,' he said insolently, 'but I don't think you'd be willing.'

His taunting words angered her, and although here was the opening she wanted, no way was she going to begin their relationship in this manner. It had to be a gradual process so that he did not realise what was happening.

If she suddenly said, 'Okay, we'll do what you want,' he would suspect her motives. So she said in a tone that matched his for sarcasm, 'You're quite right, I wouldn't, but as neither of us is entirely happy sitting here I see no point in remaining.'

She stood up and looked towards the top of the Peak. Usually at this time of day it was shrouded in mist, but this evening it was clear. 'I think I'll take a ride in the funicular,' she said, more to herself than to him.

'I'll come with you.' Vane stood up with surprising speed. 'There should be just time before dinner.'

'I meant alone,' she said determinedly.

He smiled strangely. 'I know you did, but I always think it's so much more enjoyable when you share experiences.'

Debra's brown eyes were hostile. 'It depends who with.'

'I can be quite charming if you'd give yourself a chance to find out.' He turned on the full power of his smile, hooded eyes insolently probing, and

Debra felt herself grow weak, understanding why Liz found herself so easily drawn towards him.

It fed her love, caused an ache in her heart and a longing to spill out the truth. 'If you put it like that,' she said with forced lightness, 'how can I refuse? What about Liz, though, do you think she'll mind?'

'Such concern is enchanting,' he said, 'especially when she had no compunction about leaving you.'

She stared at him hardly. It sounded very much as though he was deliberately trying to cause a rift between them. 'I don't believe that,' she said coldly.

He laughed. 'You're right, she wanted to wait.'

'But you persuaded her you'd have more fun alone?' Her eyes narrowed. It was so easy to fall out with him.

He shrugged. 'You know what they say about threesomes.'

'So you're sharing out your favours, my friend on one occasion, me the next?'

'Why not?' he said easily. 'It's by far the best solution. In that way I'll keep you both happy.'

Debra turned, bitterly angry. 'You don't have to keep me happy, Vane Oliver. I'm going for that ride, but alone. I don't want you with me, ever!'

As she walked away tears ran down her cheeks. Jealousy was a cruel disease, eating away inside her, making her say and do things she did not mean. It looked as though her plan was a non-starter, there was no way she could accept his trifling attitude.

To him it was all a game—two women at his disposal, both willing and eager for his attention. Except that unlike Liz she had to hide her feelings.

Getting him to fall for her would be catastrophic, it would be her own heart that would be broken, not his.

The ride in the cable car helped calm Debra's turmoil, and when she got out at the last station, which was still not quite at the top, she anticipated the walk ahead with pleasure.

Victoria and the harbour were spread out below like a model on a board, sampans and junks floated on the shining water, islands rose like purple hills.

She could see the tip of Vane's villa through the jungle of growth that covered the hillside, and felt thankful that she had come up here without him.

The grass was dry beneath her feet, the air cool and sweet. The odours which were so much a part of Hong Kong did not reach her and she inhaled deeply, appreciatively.

By far the best solution would be to leave the island, but unless Liz was willing there was no way she would go.

She ought to be grateful, she supposed, that her friend had pulled out of her deep depression. She would have been if it were any other man than the one she loved herself.

The irony of the situation did not escape her. It hurt, it hurt a great deal, and if there was a way out she would have willingly taken it.

As she stood deep in thought a parakeet flew, squawking, from a straggling clump of bamboo. Disturbed by the noise, bulbuls and orioles rose high into the air. Debra watched until they settled once again in the casuarinas and wild banana, and then continued her upward trek.

After a while she sank down into a grassy hollow and lay staring up at the blue sky. Her whole life had been turned upside down since Vane had brought her to Hong Kong. The job itself was simple, had he not been here too. Why couldn't he have stayed in London? Surely he had never spent so much time here before.

Perhaps, once he had convinced himself that she was able to cope, he would not remain here for such long periods.

She was kidding herself, she knew, but she needed some straw to clutch at, something to stop herself from going slowly mad.

Debra remained on the Peak for a long time, far longer than she intended, enjoying a cup of iced tea in the Peak Café garden, ignoring the grandiose Peak Tower with its three restaurants which had been built since she was last here.

Idly she watched a cat stalking a bird, admired the brilliant flowers attended by beautiful black and white butterflies.

As the rosy sun began to sink low, so too mist began to gather across the hill, pink fluffy light clouds floated gracefully. Below, the white villas and apartment blocks glowed in fairytale splendour, stained with magical colour from the setting sun.

Windows gleamed with sudden brilliance, until gradually, as the golden orb sank altogether, yellow lights began to sparkle, strung down the hillside and across the island like a necklace of diamonds.

The harbour was lit with a million glittering points of light, neon signs flashed, the city's night life was beginning.

Debra stood entranced, time forgotten. It was a spellbinding, romantic moment and she would have liked to share it with Vane.

She sighed deeply, sadly, jumping visibly when a voice behind said, 'Quite something, isn't it?'

'Vane!' She spun round, unable to control her pleasure at seeing him.

'Liz and I were worried. I had no idea you intended staying out this long.'

She smiled sadly. 'Nor did I, but it's sort of special up here, I couldn't drag myself away.'

His arm snaked carelessly about her shoulders and because she was still under the spell of the beauty that was unfolding before her eyes, she did not resist.

It was like being suspended in a different world. The floating mist was encompassing them, obscuring their view so that all they saw were tantalising glimpses of the glittering scene below.

It felt entirely natural that he should kiss her, Debra willingly raising her lips to his. It was a sweet, passionless kiss, which nevertheless filled her with heady intoxication, and her eyes shone as brilliantly as the lights below.

'I think we ought to get back,' he said gently. 'I told Liz I wouldn't be long.'

Debra was forced to agree, though reluctantly. She wanted this moment to go on and on, knowing that Vane attributed her changed mood to her surroundings, and knowing that she could get away with it without him attaching too much significance to her behaviour.

Arms about each other's waists, they made their way down to the station. They had just missed a cable car and Debra was glad of the ten-minute wait before the next.

Vane was gentle with her as she stood in the circle of his arms, pressing kisses into her hair,

remaining unusually silent as though the magic got
through to him too.

When they eventually arrived back at the villa
Liz was obviously angry. Pulling away from Vane,
Debra said lightly, 'I was watching the sunset.
There was no need to be concerned, either of you.'

Deliberately she cooled her manner towards her
employer, and saw a frown flicker before he caught
Liz's arm. 'I could do with a drink, come and pour
me one while Debra eats her dinner.'

'I should imagine it's ruined,' said her friend
sarcastically. 'Serves you right for staying out so
long.'

Debra shrugged. 'I'm not hungry anyway, I'm
going to bed. It's work tomorrow and my boss will
never forgive me if I'm late.' She could not help
what she said. Seeing Vane change his affections
so lightly hurt like an open wound, and her only
defence was to hit back.

His lips tightened. 'It's not that late, Debra.
Aren't you being a little bit childish?'

The sharpness of his voice cut deep. Her eyes
flashed angrily. 'I don't think so. My walk has tired
me out. Are you going to make an issue out of it,
or can I go?'

'Let her go,' said Liz softly. 'It's much more fun
on our own.'

And to Debra's annoyance he nodded. 'A good
idea, sweetheart—at least you and I don't fall out.'

CHAPTER SIX

THE fact that she was tired had not been an excuse, and Debra fell asleep almost as soon as she lay down, despite her disquieted thoughts, not waking until her alarm shrilled the next morning.

She lay for a few minutes, not looking forward to the drive to work with Vane. Perhaps if she hurried she might get out of the house before him and catch the railway car down.

Wishful thinking, she decided, when he appeared as she was finishing her coffee. He eyed her appraisingly, and Debra felt her colour rise.

'You look charmingly refreshed.' His gaze lingered on her face and he bent to plant a kiss on the tip of her nose. Their sharp words of last night might never have been.

She looked at him crossly. 'I was just leaving. I won't wait, if you don't mind. I fancy the walk.'

'But I do mind.' His expression darkened. 'You're being childish again. It's almost as though you're afraid of me.'

Debra controlled an impatient sigh and sat back in her seat. 'Very well, I'll wait.' Her lips were compressed and she felt far from happy.

As he saw her irritation Vane's own temper rose and he buttered his toast with quick, violent movements. Between mouthfuls he said, 'On the Peak last night I gained the impression that you'd begun to accept me. What's gone wrong?'

'That was last night,' she said acidly.

'And this morning you've changed your mind?' She tilted her chin. 'So what if I have?'

'Because it's madness. You're the most contrary creature I've ever met.' He chewed savagely and gulped down his coffee.

'What's it to do with you?' questioned Debra defensively. 'So long as I do my work properly isn't that all that matters?'

He wiped his mouth on a napkin and scraped back his chair. He was as tense as a coiled spring and Debra hated herself for hurting him, but it was the only defence she had.

One day, one day soon, when she felt she could cope, she would let him get closer, she would put into action her plan of revenge. But not yet, not while her love was so new and vulnerable and she was the one who would get hurt.

Following him out to the car, Debra wondered whether she ought to apologise, but once inside, taking a look at his stern face, she decided against it.

For as long as he made a fuss of Liz she would never feel anything else but jealous hostility. It looked very much as though her whole stay in Hong Kong would be anything but happy.

It was a relief when they arrived, and when Mr Fu told her that the new car had been delivered she felt quite lighthearted, even smiling at Vane as she listened to the news.

When the manager had disappeared he said, 'You needn't have made your delight quite so obvious. I know you find it distasteful travelling with me, but quite how much I didn't realise until this moment. Perhaps it might please you further that I intend returning to London tomorrow.'

He watched her face carefully and Debra knew he expected relief. Contrarily disappointment filled her thoughts, echoing in her eyes.

'You amaze me,' he said drily. 'I thought you would jump for joy. Aren't you pleased that I'm going?'

'What do you think?' she prevaricated. 'I was considering Liz being left on her own. Does she know of your plans?'

'You lie glibly,' he said, a harsh frown creasing his brow. 'You've made no secret of the fact that you disapprove of my friendship with Liz.'

'I do,' she said, 'but being the contrary person I am I also appreciate that you've done her good.'

'You're asking the best of both worlds,' he snapped.

'Is that too much?' she queried hotly.

'I think you know the answer to that. Get to your office, Debra, before I lose my temper altogether.'

'And lose face with your staff?' she goaded. 'That would never do, would it? Mr Oliver's a perfect gentleman, Mr Oliver never says a word out of place, Mr Ol——'

His hand against her mouth shut her up. She staggered back, tears gathering in her eyes. 'You enjoyed doing that!'

'I did.' He opened her door and bundled her inside. 'Cry your eyes out there, just make sure no one sees you.'

He was gone before she could make a suitable reply. Angrily Debra banged her fists on the desk. 'Roll on tomorrow,' she said aloud, 'the sooner he's gone the better!'

It had come as a surprise, the news that he was

leaving. When had he made up his mind? she wondered. Would it come as much as a shock to Liz, or did she already know?

A short while later he sent for her. 'Bring those designs with you,' he snapped, before the line went dead.

Debra had become used to his requests and marched along to his office, not bothering to hide her anger, aware that her face still bore the marks of her tears. She flung the sheets down on his desk and then stood back a pace and waited.

Vane said nothing, he did not even look at her, picking up the pages one by one, studying them carefully. He took so long that she began to feel uneasy. Perhaps he did not like them. Perhaps these were not the sort of things he wanted.

What if he decided she was not suitable for the job after all? The thought that he might dismiss her caused a flutter of dismay; despite everything, despite their harsh words, she still loved him, and the thought of them parting was more than she could bear.

When she could stand the uncertainty no longer she said loudly, 'If you don't like them, Mr Oliver, just say so. I can easily do some more.'

Slowly he raised his head, looking at her from beneath his thick lashes. 'I do like them,' he said. 'You've captured the very essence of femininity I was trying to create. Between us I think we'll make a good team.'

His praise did not please her as much as it might have done had things been different between them. A good working relationship was not what she wanted, not ultimately. But of course he wouldn't know that. Time and time again she had reminded him that he was nothing other than her employer, it was about time she reminded herself.

'I'm glad,' she said dully. 'I was pleased with them myself. I felt they were exactly right.'

'You don't sound very pleased.' He suddenly pushed himself up and came round the desk. 'Did you expect me to jump for joy?'

Debra attempted to smile. 'Knowing you, no.'

'But you expected more enthusiasm?'

She shrugged. 'Not really. I don't know what I expected. I'm relieved that you like them.'

'Relieved? Were you anticipating that I'd throw them back in your face? Is that what you were expecting, Debra?' His eyes held hers. 'Let me tell you one thing, I never let my private feelings get mixed up with business. No matter if we'd just had the biggest row of all time, I would still give you my honest opinion. You might do as well to follow my example.'

In other words, while they were at work he was prepared to forget any enmity between them, but back home? She gave a mental shrug. What did it matter, he was leaving tomorrow anyway.

It suddenly hit her how dull life would be without him. Liz would inevitably miss him too, but she herself would feel bereft, and the days would drag until he came back again.

He studied her intently for a few minutes, not missing the tear marks on her cheek, and she felt herself grow warm and uncomfortable. Then he swung away and opening a drawer in his desk pulled out a sheaf of papers.

'I've done a few rough sketches for my Hong Kong collection. They're nowhere near finished, but I thought you might like to look through them while I'm away, you might come up with a few ideas for accessories. We'll get together when I return, see what we can conjure up between us.'

She should have been flattered, so why wasn't she? Instead she felt on the verge of tears. With an effort she managed a weak smile. 'I'll see what I can do.'

With an impatient gesture Vane dismissed her. 'Go and try out your new car, call on some of the factories on your list. It will do you good to get out.'

Debra went without saying another word. His impending departure made her unhappy and she drove from factory to factory without being truly aware of what she was doing.

When she arrived back at the villa shortly after five Vane still had not returned. Liz looked put out, her pretty blue eyes sparking. 'Where's Vane?' she demanded irritably. 'Haven't you come home with him?'

'I have my own car now,' shrugged Debra. 'I haven't seen him all day. Has he told you about his plans to go to London?'

Liz's head jerked sharply, her eyes narrowed. 'Not a word—when's he going?'

'Don't ask me,' said Debra. 'He only told me this morning. I thought you knew.'

Unhappiness shadowed Liz's face, a mild reflection of the grief she had felt when her parents died. It was what Debra had been afraid of, afraid that she might become too involved and when the irrevocable split came find herself desperately unhappy.

One thing was clear in Debra's mind. If and when Vane returned she would make sure he did not resume his relationship with her friend. While he was away she would do her best to put Liz off him.

'I reckon we'll be well rid of him,' she said, trying to console Liz with a warm smile. 'We haven't seen much of each other while he's been around. We'll be able to do things together, revisit all the places we knew when we were kids, go on shopping expeditions.'

'When you're not working,' complained Liz bitterly. 'You don't realise how time drags when I'm on my own. When Vane came home at lunchtime it wasn't so bad. I'm not looking forward to his going, not one little bit.'

'You'll soon adjust.' Debra felt her friend was being unreasonable. 'Perhaps he'll bring back that tutor he promised you. It's about time you began your lessons again.'

'I'm fed up with schooling,' snapped liz.

'You'll never be a doctor if you don't study,' reproved Debra mildly.

Liz pulled a face. 'I'm not sure I want to be a doctor now. I'd rather like to get married instead of pursuing a career.'

And it was perfectly clear what man she had in mind, thought Debra bitterly. 'Don't be ridiculous!' she said sharply. 'You know it's what your own parents wanted. Don't let them down simply because they're not here.'

'I wonder how long Vane will be away?' said Liz, pursuing what was uppermost in her mind.

'Who knows?' shrugged Debra. 'His base is in London. We couldn't expect him to stay here very long.'

'But he likes it here,' insisted Liz. 'He told me

so. He said he wouldn't mind making it his permanent home.'

This was news to Debra, and she wondered what the attraction was. 'I shouldn't attach too much importance to what he says. I can't really see him settling out here. He has too many interests in England.'

Liz glanced at her friend angrily. 'You know nothing at all about Vane. We had some long talks together, I feel I've known him for years. Why don't you like him?'

'I've never said I don't like him,' said Debra heatedly.

'Not in so many words, but I've seen the way you look at him, almost as though you hate him. I used to think you were jealous, but now I'm not so sure. You have a good job, Deb, you can't afford not to be nice to him.'

'Is that why you're all over him?' enquired Debra with unusual sarcasm.

Liz had the grace to look ashamed. 'Shall we get ready for dinner? It doesn't look as though he's coming after all.'

But by the time Debra had changed Vane had returned. He and Liz were in the elegant drawing room, talking softly, not hearing her enter.

'It's unfortunate I have to go,' he was saying, 'but I'll be back as soon as I can. I shall miss you.'

Liz touched his cheek and was about to answer when she saw Debra. Unselfconsciously she rose. 'We were waiting for you—dinner's ready.'

Vane turned and gave her a tight-lipped smile. She grimaced in response, wishing perversely that it was herself he was going to miss. 'Is your flight fixed, Mr Oliver?' she asked coldly.

He nodded. 'Seven in the morning. This will be our last meal together for quite a while.'

'So we must make sure it's a pleasant one,' said Liz, giving Debra a warning look.

But it was difficult trying to be sociable when the man she loved devoted his attention to someone else. She might as well not have been there for all the notice they took of her. It was as though they were in a world of their own, conscious only that parting was imminent, making the most of their last few hours.

Even after dinner they sat together on the couch, talking about everything and nothing. Debra sipped the drink he poured her, growing more and more cross, wondering whether they would notice if she slipped away.

Almost as though he was aware of what was going through her mind Vane said suddenly, 'You're very quiet tonight, Debra. Can I attribute it to my impending departure?'

She looked at him steadily. 'You can, but it wouldn't be true.'

He smiled wryly. 'Then what's wrong, feeling neglected?'

Before she could answer he crossed the room and pulled her to her feet, glancing back over his shoulder. 'Liz, your poor friend's upset because I'm paying you too much attention.'

Liz shrugged petulantly, clearly not pleased that he was shifting his favours to her friend. But ignoring her now, Vane held Debra close, moving in rhythm to the soft music which filled the room.

She felt the inevitable weakness in her limbs and caring little that Liz was throwing her murderous

looks rested her head against the muscular hardness of his chest.

The music stopped and she opened her eyes. Liz
had disappeared. She looked questioningly at
Vane. He smiled and changed the record.

'Another dance, Debra? It's not often we're
alone, let's make the most of it.'

One half of Debra was delighted, the other
puzzled that he should behave like this behind her
friend's back. Heedless of the fact that it was a
prime moment to begin to put into effect her plan
of revenge Debra pulled away hotly.

'What sort of a man are you, Vane Oliver, that
you can treat Liz like this?'

He smiled strangely. 'You think she dis-
approves?'

'Isn't it obvious?' snapped Debra, wide-eyed.

He ignored her question. 'Let's not worry about
Liz. Dance with me, Debra, let me take back to
England the memory of you in my arms.' Again he
caught her close. 'You're so delicate I feel that if I
squeeze too tightly your bones will break.'

Debra had no doubt they would. He had tremendous strength, his arms were like two iron
bands about her body. She felt she ought to
struggle, deny this man the chance to embrace her,
but somehow her love flooded to the surface and
her submission was complete.

Without giving it a further thought she pressed
close, thrilled at the feel of his lithe hard body
against hers. Her heart raced painfully, blood
pounded in her head, and when his hand cupped
her breast she felt herself drowning in a tide of
ecstacy.

He led her gently towards the couch and they

lay down side by side, kissing passionately, as though their lives depended on it, his hands moving expertly over her body, caressing, teasing.

It was a long time before she thought of Liz again, and realised that Vane probably treated her in the same manner—he had in fact spent several hours in her room!

With a sudden scream she pushed him from her. 'Get away, you louse, get away! I know you've made love to Liz, but it doesn't mean you can do it to me too!'

His face hardened. 'If I were you, Debra, I'd make sure of your facts before you make accusations like that.'

'I am sure,' she cried dementedly. How close she had come to making a fool of herself, how easily he had made her forget her hostility!

Any last thoughts she had had of making him fall in love with her fled. Before she knew it she would find herself in bed with him. She had no control over her feelings when he exerted himself. She was better off having nothing to do with him at all.

If Liz chose to let Vane Oliver make love to her then she would have to face the consequences. It was the last time she, Debra, would interfere. Neither of them thanked her for it.

'I'm confident if you asked Liz she'd tell you differently.' Vane stood before her, arms folded, silver eyes shooting through her like twin knives. 'Why don't you?'

'Do you think she'd tell me?' she rasped. 'For a man who knows so much about women you're remarkably naïve if you think we discuss our love lives.'

'Some women do,' he said maliciously. 'They enjoy boasting.'

She turned away in desperation. 'Liz doesn't, neither do I. We ought both to have kept well clear of you. It's your type who can get a girl into trouble.'

His brows rose mockingly. 'I never push myself, Debra. A girl has to be willing—like you were a few minutes ago. What happened?'

'You know damn well what happened!' she grated. 'I thought about Liz. Perhaps you should too, considering the amount of time you spend with her.'

He looked at her thoughtfully. 'Would it change things between you and me if I assured you that Liz is nothing more than a friend?'

She shook her head vehemently. 'I wouldn't believe you. I prefer to believe what I see and hear. So far as I'm concerned you're a lecherous old man, and if you never come back to Hong Kong I shall be very happy.'

His face became blank, as though he had drawn a shutter over his feelings. 'I wish you hadn't said that, Debra, because I will be back. This is my villa, and even if you're not pleased to see me than I know your friend will be.'

'Liz is a fool,' she snapped. 'She doesn't know what she's doing. Why don't you tell her you're stringing her along? Why don't you be honest instead of letting her think that there might be a future in your relationship?'

'Because,' he said quietly, 'there is a future. I'm quite sure about that.'

Debra was dumbfounded. All along she had thought Liz was lying when she'd said Vane loved her. Almost paralysed with shock, she said, 'In that case there's nothing more to be said. Goodnight, Vane. I apologise if I misjudged you.'

She staggered from the room, ignoring his, 'Debra, wait, you don't understand!'

Out in the hall she met Liz, who looked at her stricken face and asked, 'Debra, what's wrong?'

Flashing her an outraged look, Debra cried, 'Ask him—it's his fault, everything's his fault. I wish we'd never come to Hong Kong. I wish I was dead!'

Liz's face echoed some of Debra's shock and she rushed into the room. 'Vane, what's happened?' The door closed and their voices became nothing more than a murmur.

Slowly Debra trailed to her room, pulling off her clothes one by one, stepping under the shower like a zombie, and eventually dropping on to the bed.

There was no point in getting between the sheets, she would not sleep. She felt as though she would never sleep again in her whole life.

As numbness faded Debra began to feel angry. They had deliberately kept their feelings hidden, tried to make her believe that they were nothing more than friends, or at least Vane had. Why? Was he afraid she might be hurt?

She was more hurt by his deception, and the fact that she too loved him. Never had she imagined it would come to this. Liz and Vane? It just didn't seem possible.

One thing was clear, no way could she live with them once they were married. If they made this their home then she would give up her job and return to London.

Vane remained in London for the next few weeks, phoning both the office and Liz frequently, but never once asking to speak to Debra. Not that she wanted him to. Occasionally a message was passed on to her regarding her job, but that was all.

One day Mai Mai came into her office, her handsome face as black as thunder. 'What's this I hear about you designing some accessories for Vane's Hong Kong collection? I've never heard of it.'

So he hadn't discussed it with his chief designer? Debra felt secretly pleased, but he had not told her that she was not to talk about it, so she said airily, 'Oh, hasn't he told you? He's doing a range for the smaller woman and he thought it would be nice to use an Oriental theme.'

Mai Mai glanced at the sketches on Debra's drawing board. 'It's unlike Vane not to tell me what he's doing. Are you sure you should be working from these? They're not finished.'

'I know,' smiled Debra, 'but he wanted me to see what ideas I could come up with while he was away, and then we'll get together on the complete range.'

If looks could kill she would have died at that very moment. Mai Mai's dark eyes were furious, her red mouth turned down angrily at the corners. 'For your information, Miss Delaney, Vane Oliver *always* discusses his ideas with me. I am his chief designer, please do not forget it.'

'You and I work in different fields,' said Debra quietly but firmly.

'Meaning what?' snapped the other woman.

'That we're both equally important to him,' supplied Debra glibly.

Mai Mai tossed her head. 'I have worked with Vane ever since he opened this branch, and I certainly do not intend to move over for someone like you.'

Enraged now by this woman's supercilious manner, Debra said angrily, 'I think the decision as to who should do his work lies with Mr Oliver himself. Maybe you'd like to carry your complaints to him?'

'I shall,' returned the Cantonese woman positively, 'just as soon as he returns.' With that she swept out of the office, banging the door so loudly behind her that the pens on Debra's desk rattled.

She was both annoyed and amused by Mai Mai's attitude. The woman had no right charging in here accusing her of doing work that she should not be doing. But if she thought there was something going on between her and Vane then she was sadly mistaken.

Perhaps she ought to tell her. It would be fun to go in and say, 'I'm not having an affair with Mr Oliver, if that's what you think, but he's going to marry my friend.'

That really would shock Mai Mai, give her something worth worrying about.

The longer Vane stayed away the more miserable Liz became, and no matter how Debra tried to bully her out of it, she spent long hours in the house, sitting beside the phone, pouncing on it the moment it rang.

After his calls Liz would be happy for a while, then her lethargy would return. It was worse, if anything, than after the accident, thought Debra. Liz was so miserable it was unbelievable.

And this purely because Vane was away for a few weeks. What would she be like if they parted altogether? Not that that was likely to happen now, thought Debra dully. All too soon they would be naming the day, and that would be the end of any faint hopes she entertained herself that he did not really love Liz, that one day he might turn to her.

He arrived back unexpectedly, and Debra returned from work to find them both out. She ate a solitary meal and went to bed early, not particularly wanting to see Vane, or at least not with Liz, not when she knew she would see the love shining in their eyes.

She had not been in bed long when she heard his car. Her heart throbbed warningly, she grew tense, unconsciously listening for sounds that would tell her what they were doing.

When she heard footsteps along the corridor she froze, fearing they were going to bed—together. Wanting to listen, yet afraid, pulling the sheets over her head, telling herself that she was overreacting.

It was not until her door opened that she realised she had heard only one set of footsteps. Assuming it to be Liz to tell her about her evening out, Debra called from beneath the sheets, 'Goodnight, Liz, I'm sorry I didn't wait up, but I have a headache.'

'Or was it because you didn't want to see me?' The sheets were jerked back, and Vane towered above her, his deepset eyes almost hidden by the frown that blackened his brow.

A tremor ran through her. 'Of course not, Vane,' she lied. 'If I'd known you'd be this early I'd have waited. I thought you'd be late, and I was tired, and——'

She faltered, uncomfortably aware that her

nightdress was revealing more than she would have liked, and that Vane was insolently studying her, not listening to her excuses.

'You have a beautiful body,' he said thickly, and reached out.

Debra snatched at the sheets with a hand that trembled. There had been desire on his face and for one reckless second she had wanted to feel his hands on her, revel in the luxury of physical contact.

But for one second, that was all. Vane loved her friend, any feelings he might have for herself were purely chemical. Any man who saw a half-naked woman in bed would react the same.

'What do you want?' she demanded passionately, unusual colour staining her cheeks.

'I wondered how you were.'

Debra averted her eyes. 'I can't really believe you feel any concern for me.'

'I've missed you,' he said, and something in the way he spoke made her look at him, and the love in her heart grew.

He exuded a masculine virility that no woman in her right mind could resist. If he chose to jump into bed with her she would say to hell with Liz, he wants me and I want him, and that's all that matters.

They disgusted her, these feelings, yet she could do nothing about them. Her mind ran riot and, afraid that her thoughts might be reflected in her eyes, she jumped out of bed, pulling a dressing gown defensively about her shoulders.

'I don't believe that,' she said flatly, 'but if you want me to join you and Liz I will.'

He gripped her shoulders, strong fingers digging

painfully into her soft flesh. 'Dear little Debra, don't be so aggressive. It doesn't become you.'

'Take your hands off!' she cried desperately, unable to bear the exquisite torture of his touch. 'If you don't I shall scream!'

His eyes narrowed. 'I don't think you will. I think you like me touching you, I can feel your anticipation.' He lowered his head. 'Have you missed me? Have you spent sleepless nights wondering when I'll be back? Is that what's wrong?'

Debra was torn. She ached for his kiss, yet at the same time despised him for betraying her friend. Loyalty won. Fiercely she struggled, managed to wrench away.

'Vane Oliver,' she demanded, 'what game are you playing? What do you think Liz would say if she saw what you're doing? Perhaps I ought to call her, let her see what you're really like!'

To her surprise he shrugged. Without attempting to defend himself he moved towards the door. 'There's a nightcap waiting for me. And I certainly need it!'

CHAPTER SEVEN

DEBRA fully expected Vane to accompany her to the office the next morning, and was surprised and disappointed when there was no sign of him.

Instead of going out on her usual rounds she stayed in, ostensibly to write reports, but in reality because she wanted to see Vane.

Her disillusionment was very real when he did not turn up. It was only too easy to guess what he was doing, and she had been a fool to let his love for Liz slip her mind.

However, when she got home she found Liz alone. 'Vane's gone shopping,' she said sulkily, 'to buy new silks for his collection. He wouldn't let me go with him.'

It was understandable, thought Debra. Liz would distract him, he would not be able to think clearly when he had his loved one at his side.

He returned later looking very satisfied with himself. 'I've succeeded in getting hold of some beautiful materials,' he said to Debra. 'Crisp satins, shimmering Thai silk, gold-embroidered chiffon. I can't wait now to get on with my collection.' For the moment Liz was ignored. 'You'll look very beautiful, Debra, modelling my clothes. As soon as the designs are finished you must come to London to be measured. Work will begin right away—I shan't risk having them made up here. I shall put my top cutters and machinists on the work. You'll be sensational.'

144

Debra had given no more thought to his earlier suggestion and she gazed at him now with horror. 'You're serious?'

'Of course. I thought it was all fixed. You're not going to let me down now?'

Even Liz looked excited. 'Fancy, you'll have your photograph in all the glossy magazines!'

Debra felt even more uneasy. 'It's not that type of work, is it? I thought I'd just be a house model.'

Vane smiled confidently. 'Naturally there'll be a great deal of interest in my new collection. Photographs are inevitable, but don't worry, you'll be given all the necessary tests. The main thing you'll have to contend with is jealousy. You'll be my star attraction, and my other models won't like it. Think you can cope?'

His smile was reassuring, it made her feel special, and warm, and wanted, and Debra nodded. 'If you have faith in me, then I'll do my best not to let you down. Is my job here finished?'

'No way,' he said positively. 'You're a permanent fixture so far as I'm concerned.'

Maybe, thought Debra. It all depended on the outcome of his relationship with Liz. At the moment no one would believe they were lovers. His eyes were for her alone, and strangely Liz did not seem to mind. Perhaps she was proud that her friend was going to be a model, albeit temporarily.

He then sprang his second surprise. 'Go and get changed, both of you, I've booked seats at the opera.'

Liz frowned, then smiled. 'Wonderful! I've had enough of stopping in.'

Quite clearly her pleasure was somewhat dimmed by the thought of Debra accompanying them, but it could not be helped. She was not going to turn down Vane's offer simply because she did not want Debra with them.

It had been a long time since Debra had been out herself. It would make a pleasant change. 'Thank you, Vane,' she said demurely, 'I shall enjoy that.'

As with all Chinese operas, the costumes and make-up were more dramatic than the acting itself, which was accompanied by incessant banging of cymbals and gongs.

'Do you find inspiration in these costumes?' Debra asked at one stage, after she had feasted her eyes on the gleaming, brilliantly-coloured silks, finely embroidered with dragons and phoenixes, and waves and clouds.

He turned and smiled, taking her small hand in his. 'You are my inspiration, Debra,' and for a moment it was as though time stood still, as though they were alone in the theatre.

Her love welled over and stretching up she kissed his cheek. 'You're very kind, Vane.'

'I could be more than kind if you'd let me.' His voice was deep and emotive and his eyes speared through her.

Had Debra not caught a glimpse of Liz's frozen face she might have forgotten herself and asked what he meant. She knew what it sounded like— and the thought was tantalising—if he had been a free man!

Her cheeks burned and she took defence in saying, 'I think you're forgetting that you are still my employer.'

His fingers tightened and she winced, but managed to wrench her hand free. She had angered him by her remark, which was what she intended.

She despised him for splitting his loyalties so easily. It was a pity Liz was so blinded by love that she could not see what type of man he was.

On the journey home Liz insisted on sitting in the back of the car, which was unusual, and Debra guessed she had been really hurt by his attention to herself.

During the days that followed Liz became quiet and subdued and would speak to no one, including Vane. When Debra tackled her about it she refused to talk, and there was something in her manner that prevented Debra from questioning her too closely.

It was obvious she and Vane had fallen out, and that it stemmed from the night of the opera, but exactly what had happened between them she had no idea, and she was hesitant to question Vane himself.

One evening, when Liz had gone to bed extra early, and Vane took Debra into his arms, kissing her with frightening passion, she said angrily, 'I don't think you're being very fair towards Liz,' and attempted to pull free.

'In what way?' he queried, taking no notice of her struggles.

'Well, you're hardly being a gentleman.'

He laughed harshly. 'I don't feel like a gentleman where you're concerned. You bring out the animal in me.'

Debra fought even more strongly. 'If Liz finds out it will be the end of your friendship.' Surely now he would tell her?

Thick brows rose caustically. 'I see no reason why what you and I do should have anything to do with Liz.'

Debra was amazed, and blazing angry. 'I wish I understood you, Vane Oliver, but I don't think I ever will. Don't you realise that you're hurting people's feelings, or is your conceit so great that you don't give a damn? You snatch what you can when you can and to hell with everyone else!'

'You're talking in riddles,' he snapped, letting her go abruptly. 'It's not often the two of us are alone, I thought you might have appreciated this opportunity to——'

'Not at my friend's expense,' she cut in. 'I'm going to see her.'

'To tell tales,' he sneered derisively. 'If that's the way you feel, pardon me for intruding. You certainly gave the impression that you found me more than a little attractive.'

'That doesn't give you the right to paw me each time we're alone,' snapped Debra. 'There are some things a woman can't help, and feeling sexually attracted to you is one of them, but being attracted is as far as it goes. I have no intention of losing my head.'

'We don't always have control of ourselves,' he said softly, menacingly, 'and it never hurt anyone to let go occasionally. What are you afraid of, Debra, me—or yourself?'

She chose not to answer, but swung round and left the room, rushing along the corridors as though all the hounds in hell were after her.

Pausing outside Liz's door to regain her composure, Debra realised that she had done the wrong thing in tearing out like that. It would give Vane the impression that she was not as immune to him as she made out.

But it was too late to worry about that now. Taking a deep breath, she pushed open the door, only to stop abruptly when she observed that her friend was asleep.

She looked pale and shadowed, and Debra felt concerned. Didn't Vane realise what he had done to her?

Reluctant to risk bumping into him again, she went to her room and picking up a magazine settled in a chair near the window. She had scarcely begun reading when Vane entered. 'Liz is asleep,' he stated abruptly. 'Why are you here—hiding from me?'

Debra shrugged. 'You wouldn't believe me if I said no.'

'You're damn right I wouldn't,' he said savagely. 'I insist that you join me.'

'And if I refuse?' she dared.

'I shall use force. There's absolutely no point in the two of us remaining in separate rooms. It's foolish.'

Debra glared. 'It would also be foolish of me to come when it's quite clear that you're after only one thing. Don't you ever give up?'

'Not when a pretty woman's involved.' Unexpectedly he smiled. 'Don't worry, Debra, you'll be quite safe. I've taken the hint.'

Other than call him a liar there was nothing she could do but agree, although it was with reluctance that she followed.

'As it's such a beautiful evening,' he said, 'how about a walk in the garden?'

She nodded. 'Anything you like.'

He looked at her sharply, suspiciously, but she was already moving towards the door.

The fountain in the centre of the courtyard spouted water through the mouth of a black marble dragon. Urns of flowering shrubs spilt their fragrance into the night. It was peaceful and beautiful, and Debra could not be angry with Vane for long.

Hong Kong had always bound her in its spell, but here, half way up the Peak, early evening lights glistening in the harbour below, the magic deepened and quite involuntarily she turned to Vane.

'Isn't this the most beautiful place on the face of the earth?'

His smile was warm and encompassing. 'When seen through your eyes, yes, when I'm on my own I guess I don't really notice.'

'Then you should,' she scolded.

'There are other things I'd rather look at,' he replied softly.

She was not facing him as he spoke, but when she turned his eyes were upon her. She went hot and weak, but managed to keep her voice steady. 'Vane, you promised!'

'I know,' he said, 'it must be this intoxicating air you're raving about. I want you, I want you desperately.'

Debra moved quickly through the gate and across the sloping lawns at the back of the villa. It was very still and very quiet and Vane was close on her heels, and she wanted him as much as he wanted her—but she mustn't, she mustn't!

She swung round desperately. 'Vane——'

She got no farther. His mouth was on hers, hungry, demanding, and with a faint cry she gave up. What point was there in fighting? It was what they both wanted, why deny herself the pleasure?

It was not until a vision of her friend lying pale and still in bed floated before her mind's eye that Debra fought to free herself.

'Liz!' she cried. 'We can't do this to her, it's not fair, it's disloyal.'

'Liz won't know,' he said softly in her ear.

'You're despicable!' she exclaimed. How could he two-time her friend like this? Even more disturbing, what sort of life would it be for Liz after they were married? He would never remain true, that was for sure.

'You shouldn't be so irresistible,' he mouthed, completely unconcerned by her protest. 'Forget Liz for a while, enjoy yourself. Life is for living, don't shut yourself in a shell.'

His lips clamped on hers yet again so that there was no way that she could answer, and after a while all thoughts of fighting fled.

Uppermost in her mind was the fact that she loved him. Why reject a few minutes' happiness? All too soon they would be nothing more than memories.

It was not until she lay in bed that night that Debra was overcome with guilt. How could she do this to Liz? she asked herself angrily. How could Vane do it?

It certainly proved what type of man he was, and she was disgusted with herself for loving him, except that love did strange things to her. When she was with him she could not help herself; it was only when she was alone that she felt remorse.

The fact that she and Liz both loved the same man saddened her, and the worst part was that Liz had won. Whatever had gone on between them could be no more than a lovers' tiff. All too soon they would make it up and then she, Debra, would be left out in the cold once again.

Sleep, when it came, was a blessing, and she woke the next morning determined to push all thoughts of Vane from her mind.

Unfortunately when he joined her at breakfast he said he intended accompanying her on her rounds.

'I think Liz would appreciate it if you stayed with her for once,' said Debra quickly.

He frowned. 'Why, what's she said?' Quite clearly he was not going to tell her anything himself about their argument.

'Nothing, but she's been looking peaky lately. I'm sure there must be something wrong. Why don't you take her out for the day? It will do her a world of good.'

'A quick about turn,' he mocked. 'At one time you would have done anything to keep us apart.'

'Things are different now,' she snapped. 'If you're not going to stay then I will. Naturally I won't expect you to pay me.'

'Naturally,' he said drily. 'But I disagree with your line of reasoning. You're going to work and that's that.'

Debra's brown eyes widened hostilely. 'You can't make me do anything.'

He inclined his head gravely. 'True, but this is one occasion when I can and will exert my authority. Your excuse is feeble, to say the least. Liz doesn't need you, she'll be perfectly all right.'

What else could she say? Debra shook her head sadly. 'Yes, boss. Anything you say, boss.'

Vane frowned in swift anger. 'Stop that!'

'But it's what you are,' she insisted. 'You're my

employer and you think that because you pay me and because I live in your house you have a right to dictate.'

'I have,' he said smoothly, 'and that's the way it will be if you insist on being unreasonable.'

Realising that to argue further was futile, Debra turned her head savagely, staring out of the window.

'Don't sulk,' he snapped.

'What else am I supposed to do,' she demanded, 'when you become the heavy-handed boss?'

He did not answer. Instead he picked up the paper that was neatly folded before him and began reading. Debra might as well not have been there.

After breakfast she went in to Liz, who still looked pale and far from well. 'Would you like me to stay with you?' she asked, deciding that if this was what Liz wanted then she would defy Vane and accept the consequences.

But Liz shook her head adamantly. 'What for? There's nothing wrong with me.'

Brave words to hide a broken heart, thought Debra, wishing there was some way she could make the girl confide. But she had tried time and time again and knew that not until Liz was ready would she discover what had gone on to cause her this unhappiness.

The day was every bit as uncomfortable as Debra had expected. With Vane at her side she felt uneasy, unsure of herself, and although they encountered no problems at any of the factories they visited she was not convinced that Vane thought she was doing her job properly.

She was relieved when he called it a day.

Liz was asleep when they got home, or pretending to be, and Debra was compelled to spend yet another evening with Vane.

Afraid he might begin another attack on her defences, she fetched a dress she was altering and sat in a corner with her needle and thread, doing her best to ignore him.

For a while he seemed content, smoking a cigar, listening to his music, sometimes looking at her, at others gazing into space, to all outward appearances totally preoccupied.

An hour passed before he impatiently pushed himself up. 'For God's sake put that away,' he said savagely. 'Don't think I don't know what you're doing, but if you think you can protect yourself from me by that piece of material you're mistaken.'

Debra pretended to misunderstand. 'Protect myself, Vane? What do you mean?'

'You know damn well,' he spat furiously. 'Put it away before I destroy it. I want to talk over this modelling assignment of yours, and I want your full attention.'

'If it's business,' returned Debra sweetly, 'why didn't you say?'

'I shouldn't have to,' he snapped.

Debra shrugged and said nothing, but folded up her sewing and placed it neatly on the table beside her.

'I'm thinking of returning to London next week,' he said, 'and I want you to come with me for a few try-on sessions.'

'But Liz,' she protested immediately. 'I can't leave her.'

He sighed impatiently. 'Naturally I wouldn't expect you to. She can come with us if she likes, I have no objections.'

I should think not, thought Debra, since you're planning to marry her. Aloud she said, 'I expect Liz would like that. Where would we live? Don't forget we let our house.'

'I'd naturally book you into a hotel,' he said drily, 'or you could join me in my apartment, there's plenty of room.'

'No, thanks,' replied Debra quickly.

'Afraid?' he mocked.

'I have enough of you here,' she said deliberately.

A quick frown, then, 'I'm sorry that's how you feel. It's a great pity.'

'If friendship was all you wanted, there'd be no problem,' returned Debra.

'Meaning you think I'm after something else?'

She smiled acidly. 'Well, aren't you? You've chased Liz and me ever since we've been here— quite unashamedly.'

'With two entirely different reactions.' The deepset eyes regarded her gravely. 'Why can't you be as approachable as your friend?'

'I'm sorry if I've disappointed you.' She returned his gaze steadily. 'But no two people are ever the same. It's as well, don't you think?'

He shrugged. 'I suppose it stops life from becoming boring.'

'But it goes against the grain when things don't go all your own way?'

The silver eyes were watchful. 'What do you think?'

'I'm sure you're not interested in my opinion of you,' she said slowly. 'I think I'll go and see if Liz is awake.'

'I want you here,' he said with sudden ferocity. 'I enjoy your company. Why do you always run away?'

'Then come with me,' she said. 'Besides, I'm sure Liz would really prefer to see you.'

'I wonder?' he said slowly, 'but if that's what you want, go and see if she's awake—I'll be along in a few minutes.'

Liz was awake, sitting up in bed, reading a magazine. 'Vane's coming to see you,' Debra told her. 'He's concerned, he thinks you must be ill.'

Her lie was rewarded by a sudden spark in Liz's eyes. 'Pass me my hairbrush and a mirror,' she said quickly. 'I can't let him see me like this.'

Being in love suited her, thought Debra. It brought a glow to her cheeks like nothing else ever had. It was a pity Vane was not so single-minded in his devotion.

'You look lovely,' she said. 'I have some good news. Vane's taking us to London for a few days.'

'It's not the fashion show already?' queried Liz sharply.

'Oh, no,' replied Debra. 'He needs me for fittings.'

Liz's rapture faded dramatically. 'In that case I shan't come,' she said flatly. 'I shall only be in the way.'

Debra had thought Liz would be delighted, was startled by her unexpected reaction. 'But you can't stay here by yourself. You must come. Vane's booking us into a hotel—you'll enjoy it, I know.'

But Liz was adamant, and when Vane came into the room Debra said quickly, 'The London trip's off. Liz wants to stay here and naturally I can't leave her alone.'

His eyes hardened and he looked from one to the other. 'Why don't you want to come, Liz?' he asked abruptly.

The girl looked hurt and Debra wished he had not been so harsh. Couldn't he see that Liz was still desperately in love with him? Did he have to treat her so coldly? Whatever had happened surely it couldn't be so bad that he could not be gentle?

Liz gazed up at him with hurt blue eyes. 'Because I like it here,' she said. 'You and Debra go, see if I care.' The last four words were muttered defensively, telling Debra that in reality it was the last thing she wanted.

And loving her friend as she did, she knew that in no way could she hurt her. Vane had done enough harm already, whether he realised it or not.

'I won't go without you, Liz,' she said warmly, sitting on the edge of the bed and putting her arm about the younger girl's shoulders. 'If you want to stay here, then I will. The fittings will have to be done some other time.'

Vane's eyes glinted in sudden anger, his lips thinned. 'What is this, a conspiracy? I think you're forgetting, Debra, that you work for me. If I tell you you're going to London then you go.'

Her chin tilted and her eyes matched his for hardness. 'I'm not going, Vane. Make of it what you will. Sack me if you like. At this particular moment Liz needs me more than you, and my loyalty is with her.'

His eyes swivelled to the younger girl. 'Do you need her, Liz? Answer me honestly. Do you want Debra to stay here with you?'

Before she could reply Debra said quickly,

'Naturally she'll deny it, but I haven't lived with Liz nearly all her life not to know what's going on inside her head.'

This was perhaps not strictly true. At one time she and Liz had been so close that often neither needed to speak to know what the other was thinking. It was only of late she had been completely baffled by Liz's behaviour.

'I'm asking Liz,' snarled Vane, 'not you. Please be quiet.'

Debra looked at her friend, who appeared on the verge of tears. 'You're upsetting her,' she cried vexedly. 'Leave her alone!'

He looked from one to the other, pivoted, and left the room.

Knowing that she had not heard the last of it, Debra shrugged off all thoughts of their next meeting, instead concentrating her attention on Liz. 'Why don't you tell me what's wrong? Have you and Vane fallen out?'

Liz shook her head, her lips clamping together, her eyes becoming blank.

'Then what is it?' insisted Debra. 'If you won't tell me I can't help.'

'Just leave me alone,' snapped Liz suddenly. 'Leave me alone. You wouldn't understand, not in a thousand years.'

Surprised by her sudden outburst Debra said gently, 'Try me, Liz. I might surprise you. You really do have me worried.'

'But you have Vane to take your mind off it,' said Liz tightly. 'Go to him, I know that's what you want. It's what you've wanted all along. I ought to have known it would never last.'

So it *was* all over between them!

Debra took Liz into her arms. 'Would you like to tell me about it?'

But the other girl pushed her away angrily. 'Get out, Debra. Go to London, go with Vane. Just leave me alone, that's all I ask.'

Liz's face was white and her rejection hurt Debra, although she had the sense not to touch her again. 'If you could only talk about it, Liz,' she implored, 'you'd feel a lot better, I know you would.'

'Talk to you!' snapped Liz. 'You're the last person on earth I'd discuss my problems with. How would you understand when you're in love with Vane yourself? You must be laughing under your hat. Pretending to sympathise, trying to make believe that you're concerned. What do you take me for, a complete idiot?'

Debra was appalled by Liz's hatred. She had never thought that Vane would split them up like this. 'There's nothing between me and Vane,' she declared, in a last attempt to placate her friend. 'Admitted, he's tried it on, but it means nothing. Vane doesn't love me, nor ever will. It's you he loves, you've told me so yourself more than once.'

Liz sank wearily back into the pillows. 'I thought he did. I was too inexperienced to know the difference.' She spoke so quietly that Debra had to bend her head to hear. 'I know now that he was merely being kind.'

'He's told you that?' Debra recalled his words that there was a future for him and Liz together.

'He told me I was making a mistake loving him.' The tears that had threatened for so long overflowed, rolling down her cheeks, falling in damp splodges on to the silk sheets. 'He—he said he was

too old for me, that very soon I'd meet someone
my own age—and that——' She broke down completely, unable to go on, and this time did not resist
when Debra gathered her to her breast.

Debra waited until the sobs had subsided before
saying quietly, 'It might seem like the end of the
world now, but in a few weeks you'll be able to
laugh. We all go through it, we all make mistakes,
thinking we're in love with some fabulous man,
whereas in fact all it is is infatuation.'

Liz clung unashamedly to her friend. 'Oh, Debra,
I'm glad you know. It's been so horrid keeping it
to myself. I wanted to tell you, but I couldn't. I
made Vane promise not to tell you either. I thought
you'd be glad, and I couldn't stand that.'

Shaking her head, Debra said, 'I wish you'd told
me sooner. I love you as if you were my sister.
Haven't you always come to me with your problems? I'd like to think you always will.' She paused,
mopping the younger girl's face with her handkerchief. 'And Vane hasn't rejected you either, I'm
sure about that. He told you what he did for your
own good, but deep down inside he'd still like to
be your friend, if you'll let him.'

Liz shook her head vehemently. 'I don't want to
speak to him, not ever. I know I'm being stupid,
but——' She wrung her hands in distress. 'You do
understand?'

Debra nodded and smiled. 'I think I do. But time
is a great healer, you'll think differently soon, and
when you do he'll be ready and waiting.'

The young girl looked doubtful.

'He will,' confirmed Debra. 'And now I suggest
you wash your face and go back to sleep. In the
morning you'll feel much better.'

Liz smiled wanly. 'Are you going to London?'

Debra shook her head firmly. 'I'm staying here with you. He can say what he likes, he can't make me go, short of carrying me every inch of the way.'

Her friend giggled at the picture of Vane carrying Debra all the way to London. 'I'm glad, Debra, but aren't you a little bit scared? He's in a filthy mood—look how he bounced out of here.'

Debra squared her shoulders. 'I can handle Vane, don't you worry. If the worst comes to the worst I simply get another job. People are crying out for people like me, don't you know that?'

Liz grinned again. 'I'm glad you know. I feel much happier already.' She swung her legs out of bed and made her way towards the dressing room. There was a tiny crease between her brows when she turned. 'Do you love him, Deb? You never said.'

Unsure whether or not to admit it, Debra struggled with her feelings for a few moments before nodding lamely. 'But don't you dare tell him, I'll murder you if you do.'

'Your secret's safe with me,' said Liz. 'Seems like we've both fallen for the same man and neither of us is going to get him.'

'The difference being,' said Debra pointedly, 'that I haven't let him see it. You'll know next time, Liz, not to wear your heart on your sleeve.'

She waited until Liz was settled before leaving the house and strolling across the sloping lawns, inhaling deeply the fresh evening air, glad that such scenes did not happen every day. She did not think she could stand them.

It was a relief that her friend had at last confided. She felt sure now that it would not be long before she returned to normal. Perhaps then she, Debra, could go with Vane, but certainly not before. No way would she leave Liz to cope with this alone.

When she returned to the villa he was waiting for her, a shadowy figure on the verandah, leaning idly against one of the posts, his cigar glowing red in the fading light.

'I want a word with you,' he said roughly.

'And me with you,' she returned, determined that he should in no way put her down.

They moved into the drawing room where Debra switched on the central light in order that she could see him more clearly.

'You had a long talk with Liz after I'd gone,' he commented, pouring himself a drink, but not bothering to offer her one.

'So?'

His eyes narrowed. 'I would like to know what you were talking about.'

Debra's chin shot up. 'It's none of your business. Since when have I had to report to you full details of all conversations I have with my friend? I'm entitled to a certain amount of privacy!'

Anger tightened his face muscles, drawing the skin tautly across his prominent cheekbones. Silver eyes glittered from beneath hooded lids. 'I have the feeling you were discussing me. And if that's the case then I want to know what was said.'

'No,' said Debra deliberately, icily. 'what Liz and I had to discuss was private.'

'But you're not disputing the fact that my name did enter the conversation?'

'Maybe,' she shrugged. 'Does it really matter?'

'I should say it matters a great deal,' he said. 'It will probably give me the answer as to whether you're coming with me to London.'

Her eyes flashed. 'I can tell you that. The answer is no. I'm staying here with Liz.'

A pulse jerked in his jaw. 'And if I say you lose your job if you defy me?'

'It will make no difference.' There was an edge to her voice that he had not heard before. 'I managed before I worked for you, I've no doubt I can again.'

There was silence for so long that Debra wondered if she ought to leave. Then Vane said savagely, 'I'll give you a week, Debra, to make up your mind. If at the end of that time you still refuse to accompany me, then you're dismissed. I've no patience with people who defy my orders.'

Debra froze inside. She felt completely alienated from Vane, as though all the tender moments they had shared had never existed. How could he be so cruel? Didn't she mean anything to him at all, not even as a good designer?

Like Liz earlier she felt like crying, but determined not to give him the pleasure of seeing her distress she said tightly, 'If that's what you want, Mr Oliver, then so be it. You may as well sack me now, because there's no way I'll change my mind. Liz means more to me than your precious business.'

Eyes like ice glittered into her own. 'I admire your sentiments, Miss Delaney, but surely you have your priorities wrong? Don't you owe it to yourself to look after your own interests? With you out of work how are you and your friend going to live? Come to think of it, where will you live? You won't be able to get your tenants out of the house until the agreement's up, you'll be lucky even then.

These people have a way of sitting tight.'

'We could stay in Hong Kong,' replied Debra defensively.

'And live in a shack, or perhaps a junk in Aberdeen harbour? Not quite what you're used to, but I doubt you'll be able to afford anything else. After I've deducted living expenses from your salary I doubt there'll be much left.'

Debra was aghast. 'What do you mean? You said accommodation went with the job.'

He smiled mirthlessly. 'Liz doesn't work for me. I never said anything about her living here for nothing.'

Absolutely furious now, Debra picked up the nearest thing and threw it. He ducked and the vase hit an ornately framed mirror on the wall behind him.

The vase broke, the mirror shattered, but she was beyond caring. 'I hate you, Vane Oliver!' she cried loudly. 'I shall be glad to leave, do you hear, glad, glad, glad, and I hope your miserable Hong Kong collection is a failure!'

Tears raced down her cheeks as she fled, but it was not until she reached the sanctuary of her room that the enormity of what she had done hit her.

God, how could she have got so carried away that she had destroyed not one but two valuable objects? Would he insist that she pay for them? Would she spend the rest of her life working to pay off her debt to Vane Oliver? It did not bear thinking about.

She flung herself down on the bed and sobbed until she was exhausted. When her door slowly opened she half expected it to be Vane come to demand his pound of flesh.

To her relief it was Liz. The girl looked scared. 'I heard you crying. What's the matter? Have you and Vane argued?'

Debra nodded sadly. 'I've done it altogether—we'll have to go now, there's no way that we can stay on.'

This time it was Liz's turn to comfort Debra. 'What have you done that's so bad? It wasn't because of me?'

'No.' Debra managed a weak smile. 'I got mad at him because he was being unreasonable and I threw a vase. Unfortunately it hit that lovely mirror—you know, the one in the drawing room. They both smashed to pieces. Oh, Liz, I'm frightened! I bet he'll make me pay for them, and goodness knows how I'll afford it.'

'I'll help,' said Liz at once. 'I'll get a job instead of going to college. We'll manage, you'll see.'

It helped, the other girl taking her side like this, and Debra was glad they were friends once again. But she couldn't let Liz give up her career. She had set her heart on becoming a doctor.

'No,' she said. 'This is something I have to sort out myself.' She lifted her chin stubbornly. 'I'll go and see Mr Oliver now, maybe if I apologise he won't be too harsh on me.' She knew she would never sleep, not knowing what he was going to do about it.

But Liz thought differently. 'Why don't you wait until he's calmed down? You might make matters worse.'

Debra was adamant. 'I can't,' she said, shaking her head. 'I'm going now, while I still have the courage.'

Resolutely she washed her face and made her

way back to the drawing room. All evidence of the accident had been cleaned away, all that remained to tell her of what had once been was the lighter patch on the wall where the mirror had hung.

Of Vane himself there was no sign.

She knew she had to see him tonight and guessed he would be in his room. She knocked, but did not wait for a reply, but pushed open the door and marched inside.

It contained Chinese furniture, as did the other rooms, but this was quite clearly a man's room, more spartan in appearance than hers and Liz's, no bottles decorating the top of the dresser, merely a comb and brush neatly placed, a folded handkerchief. His clothes were put away out of sight, only his leather mules stood by the bed.

He had clearly just emerged from the shower and was dressed only in pyjama trousers, the dark hairs on his chest springing back to life as they dried, some still pressed flat against his deeply tanned skin.

Debra felt her pulses race before she determinedly clamped down on her feelings. 'Mr Oliver,' she said, when he looked at her questioningly, 'I've come to apologise. I'm sorry for breaking that vase and your mirror. If you let me know how much I'll pay for them.'

An eyebrow quirked. 'You realise their value?'

She shrugged. 'I know they must have cost a great deal, but if I haven't all the money now then I'll pay in instalments.'

'For the rest of your life?'

'If necessary.' She was as determined as he not to give an inch.

'Then it looks as though I'll have to keep you

on. Only that way will I make sure of getting my due.'

'I wouldn't shirk my responsibilities,' she said with a toss of her head, her shining dark hair quivering with indignation.

'I'm not saying that you would.'

'But you prefer to play safe?'

'Wouldn't you?' he mocked, 'under the circumstances? You now owe me a great deal, Miss Delaney. In fact I would say that I doubt you'll ever be out of my debt.'

There was a terrifying glint in his eyes as he spoke, and Debra felt her courage begin to desert her. She began to think that Liz was right and she ought to have waited until morning, when he might not have been so merciless.

It took all her self-control to look him straight in the eye. 'That's as may be, Mr Oliver. But I'll stay until my debt's paid, in full. I shall begin by looking for somewhere cheaper to live, and then whatever it's costing you to keep me here can go as part payment.'

'My dear Miss Delaney, that will only pay what it's cost me to keep Liz. I thought you understood that. I have no objection to you remaining, though, it's convenient, especially if I want you to do some extra work in the evenings, which might be a good idea now that you're so heavily committed.'

Debra's temper reached boiling point yet again. 'You're detestable, Mr Oliver! You're the most hateful, dictatorial, overbearing, pompous man I've ever met!'

He walked towards her, propelled her to the door. 'I think you'd better leave before you throw something else. You can't afford any more bad luck.'

'Oh, *you*—' she began, but before she could finish found herself outside the room with the door firmly closed in her face.

Perhaps as well, she decided angrily. The words that had come to mind had certainly been far from ladylike!

Debra spent an unsettled night wondering whether she would have the staying power to complete the task she had set herself. Vane Oliver was a daunting character, harder than she had ever imagined. Goodness knows why she had fallen in love with him.

To her surprise the next morning Lin Dai told her that he had suddenly been called to London. A reprieve, thought Debra thankfully, and she and Liz spent the next two days quite happily, almost able to forget the huge shadow that hung over their heads, although at first Liz had been quite horrified by what had gone on.

They comforted each other and their friendship deepened, and Debra wondered why they had ever fallen out. Trust it to be Vane Oliver who had come between them!

When he arrived back at the villa he did not look in a good mood and dismissed Liz with no compunction at all. 'I have something I want to say to Miss Delaney,' he said abruptly. 'Please leave us.'

Liz looked worried, hesitated, and then left. Debra wished she hadn't. If possible Vane was looking even angrier than he had the day she'd broken the mirror. She felt uneasy and could not even begin to imagine what he wanted to discuss.

'You remember that trouble we had at Yam Ling Kee?' he said, as soon as they were alone. 'The trouble that *you* sorted out?'

She nodded. 'Of course. They were most apologetic. Why, what have they done now—not the same thing again, surely?'

He took a deep breath and his eyes flashed like two balls of fire. 'The market's flooded with those dresses,' he bellowed. 'The ones we returned. Don't you know what this will do to my reputation? They're not me at all.

'You're sacked, Miss Delaney, fired, from this moment. Forget your debts, forget everything. Pack your bags and get out. I never want to set eyes on you again!'

CHAPTER EIGHT

DEBRA stared at Vane aghast. She could not imagine how this had happened. The manager at Yam
Ling Kee had been most apologetic about the mistake, had assured her that the Vanoli labels would
be cut out before they sold them elsewhere.

'You must be mistaken,' she said. 'They confirmed that they would do nothing with those
dresses, not with your label in. I'll go over straight
away and find out what's happened.' She looked
quickly at her watch; she might just catch them
before they finished for the day.

Vane's eyes narrowed in his hard face. 'You will
not. You're not working for me any longer. I shall
go myself, and when I return I want you gone.'

He swung round and left the room, disapproval
in every line of his body.

Debra was devastated. Vane was being unfair. It
was not her fault that these dresses had got on to
the market. So far as she was concerned the matter
had been settled satisfactorily. If it was anyone's
fault it was the Yam Ling Kee Company's.

She compressed her lips tightly. No way was she
going to take the blame. Without stopping to think
she raced after her employer, only to see his car
disappearing round the bend.

Undaunted, she fetched her keys and got out her
own vehicle. She arrived at the firm only minutes
after Vane.

He was talking animatedly, gesticulating freely,

his face an angry red, although it was quite clear by the manager's expression that he had no idea what Vane Oliver was talking about.

When he saw Debra Vane snapped, 'For Pete's sake explain to this man what's wrong. He's looking at me as though I'm some kind of moron!'

Quickly and precisely Debra outlined the situation. Mr Ho shook his head, puzzled. 'The dresses were never returned to me. I presumed they were still being held by Vanoli.'

When Debra translated Vane said angrily, 'I intend getting to the bottom of this. There's something funny going on here. Ask if I can use his telephone.'

But when he got through to London it was the middle of the night. There was nothing he could do until tomorrow.

They left the factory together. 'Do I take it,' questioned Debra, pausing beside her car, 'that I'm to get a reprieve until this thing's sorted out?'

He stared at her absentmindedly. 'What? Oh, yes, it looks as though you weren't to blame after all.'

When Debra returned Liz was anxiously waiting. 'What's going on? Why did you both rush away? Where's Vane now?'

Debra shook her head, sighing unhappily. 'There's trouble. Seems like some dresses have got on to the market with Vanoli's label in them, only they weren't Vane's designs. He's furious, and I don't blame him.'

'He was shouting at you,' persisted Liz. 'What have you got to do with it?'

Debra shrugged. 'He thought it was my fault. A good job I went along or he'd still be arguing now.' She smiled wanly. 'He sacked me, did you know?

Just like that, without even waiting to get the true picture. He said he'd forget about my debt so long as I got out of his life.'

'The swine!' said Liz angrily.

'It's all right now,' Debra assured her quickly. 'He's found out it had nothing to do with me. Mind you, if I hadn't been angry enough to follow him we'd both have been out on the streets. How do you fancy a shack on the hillside?'

Liz said, 'It might have been better than living with *him*. I can't see why I ever thought I was in love with him—he's a pig!'

Debra smiled. At least some good had come out of the situation. Liz had got over Vane far quicker than she had thought possible.

She was woken in the early hours by the sound of his voice raised in anger. She went to her door and listened. He was on the telephone and judging by the way he shouted was not getting any satisfaction.

Should she offer him her support? she asked herself. But considering the foul mood he was in she knew very well that he might once again heap the blame on her shoulders.

Back in bed, she strained her ears until the sounds of his voice ceased, and then she fell back into a deep sleep.

By morning Vane had gone. A short note on the breakfast table told her that he had left for London, undoubtedly deciding that the matter could best be resolved in person.

Debra phoned the airport, discovered that the London plane did not leave until ten, and decided to try and catch it herself.

She felt as guilty as if she really had been the one to cause all this trouble, and considered the least she could do was help Vane sort out his problems.

Not stopping to think that he might not want her, she flung a few clothes into her case, and leaving a message with Lin Dai for the still sleeping Liz, went racing out of the villa.

Never before had she driven so fast through the streets of Hong Kong, blaring her horn almost continuously. Once she reached the tunnel she made better time and boarded the plane only minutes before it took off.

Vane was not pleased to see her. 'What the devil are you doing here?' he demanded, when she planted herself in the seat next to him.

'I want to help.'

'I've had all the help I want from you,' he growled, and ignored her for the rest of the flight.

Sixteen hours is a long time to be ignored. At first Debra told herself she did not care, but as the hours lengthened she began to feel angry, and by the time they reached Gatwick she was furious.

Nevertheless, all through Customs she tagged along behind him, and when he climbed into a taxi she stepped in as well, ready with her answer if he said anything. But he merely glared and then pretended that she was not there.

She had thought he would take her to a hotel, and was amazed and a little afraid when the taxi stopped outside an impressive block of flats.

'Is this where you live?' she dared to ask.

He nodded curtly. 'If you persist in following me around then you can stay here as well.'

For the first time Debra wavered, but she realised that if she didn't stay she would lose track of him. She lifted her chin in characteristic determination. 'That's all right with me.'

His apartment was as luxurious as his villa, modern and antique furniture blending beautifully. The first thing he did was pour himself a tot of whisky.

'If you want anything to eat or drink, help yourself,' he said. 'The kitchen's through there and you can use this bedroom,' indicating a door next to the one he had just opened. 'I'm going to get some sleep.'

Debra made herself a cup of chocolate and then went to bed herself. It was still only shortly after nine, but with no one to talk to what was the use of staying up?

She slept only fitfully, aware of Vane in the next room. She was not afraid, he probably hated her after all that had happened, but even so her own love still grew and it was difficult to erase him from her mind.

To her chagrin Vane had already left when she got up the next morning. She had been so tired in the end that she had overslept, and now she was annoyed with herself for letting him go without her.

She assumed he would go to his fashion house and without even stopping for anything to eat, she hopped on to a bus and was there within a half hour of waking.

But in answer to her queries no one knew where Vane Oliver was. He had been in, she was told, but had gone tearing off again in a great hurry and in a flaming temper.

Which wasn't unusual, thought Debra. Hardly a day had passed since she'd met him that he hadn't been in a mood of some sort.

On an impulse she went to Vanoli's despatch department and enquired if anyone knew what had happened to the consignment that should have gone back to Yam Ling Kee.

Mr Brown, the manager, looked at her strangely. 'Mr Oliver's asked us the same question a dozen times. What's wrong, doesn't he believe us?'

'He doesn't know I'm here,' explained Debra. 'I'm trying to help, a new line of thought, you know.'

Mr Brown shook his head as though he thought her out of her mind. 'It went to the airport so far as I know. I can't tell you more.'

'Do you have a copy of the despatch note?' she persisted.

Grumbling beneath his breath, Mr Brown eventually produced the required document. Debra thanked him profusely and then rashly hired a taxi to take her to the airport.

But here she met with a blank. No one, it appeared, knew anything about it. Their lists had been checked thoroughly following visits by Mr Oliver himself, the consignment had never reached them.

In her role of private detective Debra now deduced that the dresses must have gone missing somewhere between Vanoli and the airport. That could involve only one man—the driver of the vehicle who had collected them.

Intuitively she decided that he had keenly summed up the situation; perhaps he'd been talking to some of the workers in Vanoli's despatch department, and decided that he could make himself a pretty packet out of selling the dresses somewhere on the black market.

By now it was long past lunchtime and Debra was starving. She ate a sandwich and drank coffee in the airport cafeteria, at the same time studying the piece of paper Mr Brown had given to her.

The driver's signature was far from decipherable,

but in the end she decided it was Hampshire. Finding her way to the unloading bay and by making a few discreet enquiries amongst the drivers themselves, she discovered that they did have a driver by the name of Lancashire, but that he had left and no one knew where he was now working.

'How about his address, doesn't anyone know where he lives?' she insisted.

The drivers smiled amongst themselves. 'Persistent young lady, aren't you?' said one of them. 'Friend of yours, is he?'

She shook her head. 'Not really. He picked up a parcel for me and it never arrived at the other end. I thought he might remember it, that's all.'

The man frowned. 'You a copper, by any chance?'

Debra laughed. 'Do I look like one?'

He seemed relieved. 'No, you're too tiny, I suppose. Let me give you a bit of advice, miss. If I was you I wouldn't probe too deeply, you know what I mean?'

'No, I don't,' returned Debra sharply. 'Are you trying to tell me that this man Lancashire has been in trouble with the police?'

His face shuttered. 'I'm saying no more. Now, if you wouldn't mind, we have work to do.'

Debra was left alone, but as she walked slowly back to the taxi rank she began to feel that she was getting somewhere.

If this man really was a criminal oughtn't she to go to the police with her suspicions? Or had Vane already done that? Best to go back to his apartment, they could pool their information and see what they came up with.

She had a long wait before he returned and he

did not look too pleased to see her still there. 'Why did you go without me this morning?' she snapped; hanging around had done nothing for her temper.

He inserted his key into the lock, shaking his head savagely. 'I decided I could sort things out better on my own.'

'Thanks for thinking I couldn't help,' she said icily.

He looked sceptical. 'You think a slip of a thing like you can succeed where I've failed?'

'What has stature got to do with it?' she demanded haughtily. 'As a matter of fact I've found out something that might interest you—assuming your enquiries have so far revealed nothing.'

'Not a thing,' he said tersely. 'The dresses disappeared somewhere between my works and the airport, that's all I know. Every line of enquiry has drawn a blank. Even the people who are selling the dresses seem unable to tell me where they bought them from, not that that's surprising. They must have thought they were on to a good thing.'

It did not seem to register that she had said she could help. She looked at him coolly. 'I know who did it.'

'You what?' He took her shoulders and shook her. 'You know, yet you're standing there as though it's of the least importance? For God's sake tell me quickly!'

The pressure from his fingers hurt. She shrugged free. 'It's a man by the name of Lancashire.'

Vane looked suspicious. 'Where does he live? How do you know? Why didn't you tell me straight away?'

'You didn't give me a chance,' she said, attempting to laugh.

Impatiently he backed away, at the same time watching her closely, fingers curled in his palms.

'He's the driver who picked up the goods.'

'How the hell?' he demanded. 'I've been to the airport myself, and they had no trace of the consignment.'

'I know,' said Debra, 'but I used my feminine wiles and had a word with some of the other drivers. I think they're shielding him. He's left the company now, but they mentioned the police. It's my guess he's done this sort of thing before. They told me not to probe.'

Vane's eyes narrowed. 'Where does he live?'

'That's the trouble,' admitted Debra. 'No one knows, or at least they're not talking. I think we ought to go to the police.'

'You're dead right,' said Vane immediately. 'I'll phone them at once—no, better still, I'll go and see them.'

'I'll come with you.'

'No, it's too much, you look all in. Wait here, I won't be long.'

He was gone before she could argue and she slumped back into her chair, too tired to insist. She fell asleep almost immediately.

When she awoke she was in bed—and completely naked! She went hot with embarrassment.

Her clothes were nowhere in sight, so draping a sheet about her limbs, she went in search of both them and Vane.

She found him in the kitchen, a pot of coffee before him, a much more relaxed expression on his face.

Almost afraid to look at him, she said, 'It wasn't

necessary to undress me completely, Vane. My top clothes would have done.'

He smiled insolently. 'The pleasure was all mine, dear lady.'

I bet it was, she thought, saying angrily, 'And I hope that's all you did do, Vane Oliver. I'm not sure that I trust you.'

His smile widened. 'You mean you can't remember?'

So he had done something else! Had they made love? Her face flamed at the thought and she shook her head slowly.

'You have a beautiful body,' he said deliberately.

She flung away, sickened. 'You're disgusting and I hate you! I wish I'd never come here.'

'You do?' Amusement lightened his eyes. 'I can't think why. I'm certainly glad you came, you've done me a power of good.'

She preferred to ignore him. 'Where are my clothes?'

'Give me a kiss and I'll tell you.' Devilish humour softened his face.

'Keep your hands off!' she snapped. 'I'm here to help, not to——'

'But you have helped,' he cut in wickedly. 'Here, have a cup of coffee and I'll tell you all about it.'

Debra had no intention of listening to what had happened during her hours of sleep, it was something she preferred not to dwell on. 'I'd like to get dressed,' she said tightly.

'As the lady wishes. Your clothes are in the bathroom. Need any help?'

She flashed him a look of hot anger, forgot the sheet, and tripped. In her haste to save herself she let go and found herself once again without covering.

In a split second Vane was helping her up.

'I can manage,' she said quickly, loudly. 'Don't touch me.'

'That isn't what you said last night,' he said quietly.

'What I did in my sleep I can't be responsible for,' she snapped. 'But as I'm now very much awake and know exactly what I'm doing, I'd thank you to leave me alone!'

In actual fact her skin tingled at his touch and she wanted nothing more than to be held close, to feel the vibrant beating of his heart, the virile strength in those lean limbs.

He had a power over her that was difficult to control. Her love, which she tried to forget, went so deep she was in grave danger of giving herself away.

Only by struggling and fighting her own inner feelings could she hold on to her self-respect. If she admitted her love there was no way that she would ever hold up her head in front of him again.

But despite her insistence Vane would not let her go. He pulled her carefully to her feet, his arms curving gently about her body, holding her firmly against him. His breath was warm in her hair and she closed her eyes, willing him to let go, fighting her instincts to respond.

When one hand cupped her chin, tilting her face towards him, her eyes flickered open, saw the desire flaring, and was afraid. They studied each other for several long seconds, each wanting but both hesitant to make the first move.

Debra licked her suddenly dry lips and it was

like an invitation. With a groan Vane lowered his head and his mouth possessed hers, gently at first, but as he realised her response, his passion increased.

She pressed closer, arching her body convulsively. It was not until he picked her up and carried her into the bedroom that she realised precisely where all this was leading.

'No, Vane,' she said in anguish. 'Please, no!'

He looked at her, silver eyes pained. 'But you want me as much as I want you. Why deny yourself the pleasure?'

'Because it wouldn't be right. You're merely taking advantage of the situation. It's a chemical reaction, no more.'

His eyes shuttered, his face became masklike. 'You could be right,' he said bluntly. 'Just bear in mind, Debra, that a man with less self-control than I have wouldn't stop now, especially knowing that deep down you want to make love.'

He swung round and left the room, and a few seconds later she heard the door of his apartment open and close.

She showered and dressed quickly, and it was not until she had made herself a cup of tea and a slice of toast that she realised he had not told her what had happened as a result of his visit to the police.

He had seemed in a better mood, that was for sure. Perhaps good had resulted.

She had taken only one bite out of her toast when he returned. His face was coolly remote, but not angry.

He joined her at the table and she poured him a cup of tea. 'What happened at the police station?'

she ventured, when it became evident he was not going to volunteer the information.

'They're looking into it,' he said. 'They know the man, he's apparently done this sort of thing before. But even if they catch him it won't help me. It's too late.'

'We could try and find out which shops have the dresses,' she said, 'and prevail on them to cut out the labels.'

Vane raised his brows. 'Theoretically a good idea, but think how many shops could be stocking them by now. It's not only London we have to think about.'

She nodded slowly. 'Perhaps it won't do as much harm as you think. *You* know they're not your particular style, but other people might not.'

He snorted derisively. 'If they have any intelligence they'll know. I'll put a notice in the trade press, it might help, but I doubt it.'

He swallowed his tea quickly and stood up. 'I'll book you on a flight back to Hong Kong. There's no point in you remaining now matters are solved. I'm grateful for what you've done, but there's no need to neglect your job.'

In other words, while she was here she was not earning the money to pay off her debt. She swallowed the sudden constricting lump in her throat, determined not to let him see her frustration. 'I'm glad I could help,' she said huskily. 'I'll go and get my things together.'

In no time at all, it seemed, she was back at the villa, only to discover to her horror that Liz had grown tired of waiting for news and flown over to London herself. They must have crossed in midair.

Panic took over. Liz wasn't used to organising things for herself. She could land in trouble. Frantically Debra telephoned Vane.

'Liz is on her way,' she told him desperately. 'You must do something, she's never travelled alone before. Her flight's due in at Gatwick at any time now.'

He muttered something that sounded suspiciously like, 'Women!' and then said, 'I'll check. If I'm not too late I'll go and meet her.'

The line went dead and the day passed slowly after that. Debra was afraid to go to sleep, tired as she was, and even Lin Dai's assurance that she would wake her if the phone rang made no difference.

It was after midnight when she heard. It was Liz herself on the line. 'Deb!' she cried. 'I'm sorry, but I'm all right, I'm at Vane's flat.'

'Why did you do it? Why didn't you stay here?' demanded Debra more sharply than she intended. 'I've been so worried!'

'How do you think I felt?' returned Liz. 'You never let me know what was going on. I had no idea where you were or anything, I couldn't wait any longer. I'm sorry if I've been a nuisance.'

'It's my fault,' admitted Debra. 'I should have phoned you, but things were so hectic I never thought. What are you doing now, coming back?'

There was a slight pause before Liz said, 'I'm staying with Vane for a while. It's all right, there's nothing like that now. We're friends, good friends, like you said we would be.'

And with that Debra had to be content.

A day or two later Lin Dai said excitedly, 'It is the Cheung Yung festival on Saturday. Will Mr

Oliver be back? He usually allows us to use the courtyard for feasting and drinking.'

'Cheung Yung?' frowned Debra, trying to remember. 'Isn't that when everyone takes to the hills to fly kites?'

The housekeeper nodded enthusiastically. 'The Peak will be crowded, it's great fun. Oh, I do hope Mr Oliver will be back in time.'

'Even if he's not,' said Debra, 'I'm sure he won't mind you doing whatever it is you usually do. Carry on, I'll take the blame if he objects.'

She could vaguely recollect from her childhood the excitement of this one of the many festivals celebrated by the Chinese.

It was always held on the ninth day of the ninth month, called the Double Ninth, and was in memory of a family who heeded the advice of a monk and climbed to the top of a mountain on a certain day to avoid disaster. When they returned to their house they found it completely destroyed and all the livestock dead.

Thousands of people would climb the Peak, and there would be sideshows and picnics and the inevitable kite-flying. She suddenly wished that Vane would be here to share in the fun.

On the Friday she had a phone call from Liz, an excited Liz. 'Guess what, Deb, I've met a super boy—he wants to be a doctor too. We're both hoping to go to the same college. I think I'm in love, really in love this time. It's nothing like what I felt for Vane.'

Debra smiled to herself. Liz still had a lot to learn. 'I'm glad,' she said. 'I'm really happy for you.' There was nothing else she could say. 'I take it from that that you won't be coming back here?'

'No,' cried Liz animatedly. 'I'm staying at Vane's flat. He says I can make it my home as long as I like. Isn't that kind of him?'

Very kind, thought Debra bitterly. It looked as though Liz had already forgotten how hateful Vane had been over the broken vase and mirror. It was only she, Debra, who remembered. She was the one who had got to work for more or less nothing so that she could pay for them.

She added a few more words of encouragement and then hung up. It was going to be an even bigger burden to bear alone. She suddenly wondered whether she would be able to go through with it.

The next morning stalls were erected in the courtyard and the grounds were alive with people both young and old, all joining in the festivities with true spirit.

Debra took the crowded funicular to the top and watched with interest the antics of two enormous bamboo and paper kites emblazoned with fierce red dragons. The object was to either cut the string of the other kite or knock it sideways in a deadly spin.

A plane flew overhead, coming in to land at Kai Tak Airport, and the kite became caught in its jet-stream, putting a sudden end to the animated battle.

It began to grow dark and still she sat there. One or two children remained, playing with their kites, shouting, laughing, thoroughly enjoying themselves.

When a shadowy figure approached and sat down beside her she felt a tingling awareness. She did not have to look to know who it was. 'Liz never said you were coming,' she said faintly.

'I wanted to surprise you.'

'I gave permission for your grounds to be used during the festival. I hope I did right.' She sounded breathless.

Vane made no comment, saying instead, 'What did you think of Liz's news?'

'I'm very pleased for her,' she said tightly, 'though I doubt it will last. She's too young to know her own mind. There was a time when I thought that——' She turned away, unable to face him.

He took her chin between firm fingers. 'When you thought what?' His silver-grey eyes held her own and she knew that if she lied it would show on her face.

'That—you and Liz—were in love.'

He chuckled. 'Liz thought she was, and I must admit I found her a very attractive little thing. Very co-operative, which is more than I can say for you. Only her innocent blue eyes saved her, I'll confess. No way could I violate the trust she put in me. We're good friends now, I'm glad to say, and I'd like to take credit for helping her find herself after her deep personal tragedy.'

'You certainly did that,' said Debra weakly, 'with a vengeance. I suppose I do have to thank you, but I heard you go to her room one night and you were a hell of a long time—are you trying to tell me that nothing happened?'

He grinned. 'You wouldn't believe me if I told you what we were talking about.'

'Try me,' she suggested.

'We were discussing you.'

Her eyes widened.

'See, I knew you'd question it. I was trying to

persuade Liz to tell me why you always held me at a distance, why you always insisted that I was the boss. You see, I knew you were physically attracted and I couldn't understand why you kept me at arm's length.'

'And what did she say?'

He shrugged. 'She still thought herself in love with me at the time, she would say nothing. I came out of that room no wiser than when I went in. Suppose you tell me—now—what it is that you've got against me?'

Debra felt herself grow warm, but attempted a careless shrug. 'Let's say I don't approve of mixing business with pleasure.'

'Not even when you love your boss?'

Her mouth fell open. 'How did—oh, I know, Liz! She had no right to tell you. I suppose you forced it from her?'

He smiled and shook his head. 'She told me freely. I reckon she thought I'd done her a good turn, so she'd do me one. I appreciated it.'

I bet you did, thought Debra, embarrassment flushing her face. Wait till she spoke to Liz again, she'd soon tell her what she thought of her! She had no right interfering. She had promised.

'You look annoyed,' Vane said softly. 'Don't blame Liz. I'm glad she told me, if she hadn't I'd have never found out.'

'What difference does it make,' said Debra tightly, 'except that now you know how hard it will be for me to go on working for you year after year. I wish I could win the pools or something, then I could pay off my debt in full and get away before you break me altogether.'

'I'd never do that,' he said thickly. 'I love you too much.'

She thought she had misheard him. Slowly and wonderingly she lifted her head, looking into the depths of his silver eyes, and what she saw made her breath catch in her throat.

'Vane?' she said faintly, questioningly.

He nodded. 'It's true, for a long, long time. You were the one who was doing the heartbreaking.' He gathered her to him with a groan, their lips met, and Debra felt her love swell and grow, and she clung to him desperately, never wanting to let him go.

'Why didn't you tell me?' she whispered.

'I could ask the same of you.' His lips moved like a trail of fire down her throat.

'Is that why you insisted I stay to pay off my debts?' Realisation had dawned.

'Mmm,' he said, busily nibbling her ear lobe. 'I had to think of some way of keeping you here. I couldn't have cared less about that damned mirror.'

'But you sacked me when you thought I'd made a mess-up over those dresses.'

He paused, smiled ruefully. 'I always say things I don't mean when I'm in a flaming temper. It's a good job you insisted on following, or I might never have discovered that you love me.'

There was silence for a while as they satisfied their mutual longings. The Peak became shrouded in mist, and Debra felt as though they were in a world of their own.

'When did you discover you loved me, Vane?'

He smiled wickedly. 'The day you walked into my office and applied for the job.'

She was surprised, and showed it. 'But why did you insist on bringing me here?'

'Because I wanted to get you alone. Unfortunately you insisted on dragging along your little friend. That was something I hadn't accounted for. I'd thought to sweep you off your feet and make you my wife almost before you knew what was happening, but somehow Liz got in the way.'

'I'm sorry,' she whispered. 'And I really thought you were going to marry her. I remember you saying one day that there was a future in your relationship with Liz.'

'My future was with you, my darling, and will be to the end of time.' He kissed her again, and it was a long time before they dragged themselves up.

'There is one thing that still bothers me,' said Debra, as they made their way down to the funicular. 'That time in your flat when you put me to bed, did you—'

He grinned wickedly. 'My darling sweetness, I couldn't do that, not to you—what do you take me for?'

'But you insinuated ...'

'And it worked.'

'Oh, I hate you!' she cried, pummelling her fists against his chest.

'No, you don't,' he said confidently, gripping both wrists with one hand and tilting her face towards him with the other. 'You're going to love me for the rest of your life—and that's an order!'

A CITY OF CONTRASTS

Although Hong Kong has been a British colony for almost a century and a half, it is truly a city of the East, with all the allure of the Orient. Situated on one of the world's most beautiful natural harbors, a mile-wide strip of the South China Sea, it is sandwiched between Hong Kong Island on the south and Kowloon Peninsula, which borders mainland China, on the north. More than four million people live in this small area—an average of more than 10,000 in each square mile!

Sailing into Hong Kong harbor, one is immediately struck by the vivid contrasts. Elegant yachts and ocean liners compete for the right of way with tiny sampans and Chinese junks bringing cargoes of fish from the South China Sea.

The setting sun casts an eerie orange light across an army of white skyscrapers in the financial district, waiting stiffly at attention below the cloud-enshrouded hump of Victoria Peak on Hong Kong Island, but nestled among these towers are the red-tiled roofs of Bhuddist pagodas!

As the sky continues to darken, the lights come on in thousands of high-rise apartments in residential Kowloon across the harbor; and the smells of Chinese cuisine are wafted on the warm breezes.

Then, while some partake of cocktails in spacious villas on the hillsides overlooking the city, thousands of others begin to throng the more than forty open-air markets. For the markets are the "poor-man's nightclubs." There the customers will socialize, eat, drink and, as often as not, gamble at such Chinese games as Mah-Jongg.

All in all, Hong Kong is a city of mystery, fascination and startling surprises. No wonder Margaret Mayo chose such an exotic setting!